THE KILLING EXPERIMENT

The Killing Experiment

by

John Newton Chance

Dales Large Print Books
Long Preston, North Yorkshire,
BD23 4ND, England.

British Library Cataloguing in Publication Data.

Chance, John Newton
    The killing experiment.

    A catalogue record of this book is
    available from the British Library

    ISBN   1-84262-359-1 pbk

First published in Great Britain in 1969 by Robert Hale Ltd.

Copyright © John Newton Chance 1969

Published in Large Print 2005 by arrangement with
Robert Hale Ltd.

Dales Large Print is an imprint of Library Magna Books Ltd.

Printed and bound in Great Britain by
T.J. (International) Ltd., Cornwall, PL28 8RW

ONE

1

As I looked back on it there is an odd feeling that I never went to Karen, that Karen came to me. Came into the house, flooded it, darkened it, frightened the air out of it.

In a sense it was there all the time, hiding in the complicated layout of my grandfather's estate. As befits the estate of a one time head of a private banking house, his wealth had been widely invested. There were many items.

There were also regular payments out of the estate made to servants of the firm to be paid as long as they lived.

Therefore I never really noticed the annual item marked 'Karen £400'. It was when it said 'Karen £849' that I thought, what an odd sum.

So when I rang Cutts, the solicitor, about something or other I added, 'Who's Karen?'

'Karen?' he said and sounded blank. Then he looked around a bit and I heard paper rustling. When he came back, he said, 'It's not who, it's what.'

'What?'

'Yes. It's a country lodge you own in the Black Forest.'

'Nobody told me,' I said.

'As you know, we're still straightening all this up. It's a lot. The smaller items may take years.'

'Where is this place?'

'A village called Mauric. It's not very big, according to this – the house, I mean. Your grandfather's retreat, I imagine. It was a gift from a firm in Munich – let me see – Faber Metalfabrik AG. After the first war your grandfather's bank lent it enough to set it up again. The loan was repaid in 1930 and this house given. That's it. You pay the upkeep. Somebody looks after it, Johann and Gertrude Stein.'

'It's empty?' I said.

'It is now, pending a decision on what to do about it. Until a short time ago it was rented on a long lease to a Doctor Frankenstein.'

'That sounds good.'

'He's gone now. Did you want to talk this over sometime? I've got details here of a sort.'

'I think I'll go and see it.'

'That's better of course. The agents are Humm, Bormann with an agent in the village who employs the Steins.'

So that was how Karen appeared. It was not surprising. Since I had inherited the rambling and it seemed – deliberately – obscure estate surprises had constantly been turning up. Unexpected ownerships, and odd investments had turned up and now Karen.

I first saw it in a storm. Some storm it was, with lightning burning the peaks of the night mountains and the rain coming down like Saturday night in the Car wash. On the road I stopped three times because even fast speed on the wipers couldn't clear the sheets of descending water.

Then I came alongside a wall, quite high, which I had been told to look for, and came to a pair of old, highly scrolled iron gates with a cast iron plate saying, 'Karen'.

I didn't bother to get out but just sat there letting the rain wash on down. Several times I saw the house blaze up out of the darkness in a blue lightning glare.

It stood amongst a lot of trees, it seemed. There were no lights on. But looking back along the road to the village, no lights showed there either.

The storm had blown the circuit breakers out.

My wait was about twenty minutes before the deluge eased. When it did I got out and opened the gates. They grounded in badly kept verges either side which had buried the iron catches.

I drove up to the house. It was about fifty

9

yards, no more. The house wasn't big, as Cutts had said, but it was ornamented like a Bavarian toy.

In the headlights the overdone woodwork and sparkling little diamonds of the window panes made the whole thing look like The Gingerbread House.

I wouldn't have been surprised to have been beckoned in by the witch.

When I switched off there was just a growling of thunder in the mountains and the heavy dripping of rain from the trees. I took my big torch off the car seat, got out and went to the door.

It was unlocked, which was not surprising, as I expected the village agent to be there, though I had seen no car outside.

The door led straight into a big room with a lot of polished wood furniture standing around.

A woman was sitting at a long table, just sitting there in the darkness, apparently thinking. She did not look round at once when my beam circled her, but when I dropped the light a bit so as not to dazzle, she looked round.

'Sprechen sie English?' I said.

'Yes,' she said.

'Good. I don't sprechen much Deutsch. Are you Mrs. Stein?'

She stood up then. She was a magnificent woman, of about thirty, a splendid figure and rich brown hair piled up behind her head rather in an Edwardian style. She was ugly, with rather coarse features, but even in the downlight of the torch, immensely attractive.

'No. I am your agent, Lilli Braun.'

We shook hands, I remember. She had a kind of regal pose as if she had meant me to kiss it. She watched me all the time with very light green eyes that gleamed in the torchlight.

'You are sitting in the dark,' I said. 'Are there no candles?'

'I was waiting for the light to come back,' she said. 'I do not mind the dark. It helps one to think.'

There was an odd tone in her voice.

Lights flickered in various parts of the room, then came on steadily. There were half a dozen, softly shaded which made the dark wood of the furniture look darker.

But it wasn't a tidy place. There were books lying around, rumpled cushions, glasses standing about on a kind of dresser.

As if someone had just got up and gone out, leaving everything.

'The Steins look after this, I understand?' I said.

She smiled.

'The Steins have not dared come here for the last few weeks,' she said.

'What?'

'The whole village has given it the go by. Your tenant was too frightening for them.'

'But he lived here for many years,' I said.

'He changed. It was very sudden.'

'Went mad, do you mean?'

'You have a story of Dr. Jekyll and Mr. Hyde,' she said.

'He changed himself?' I said. 'What kind of a doctor is he?'

'A chemist, I suppose you would call it,' she said. 'I will show you.'

She led the way out of the room and upstairs. There was a room above it as big but in what a state!

There were a lot of tables and benches and they were all covered with bottles of coloured liquids and powders, test tubes, retorts, Bunsens, distilling tubes, electronic measuring instruments – the whole gamut of a horror film lab.

The once black, polished floor was burnt and spotted with chemicals, and close under a central table, where most of the work appeared to have been done, there were scattered sheets of paper.

The lights in the room had had their shades removed and there were four or five anglepoises standing about the benches like futuristic swans, shedding bright light from their tin mouths.

I shone my torch down on the sheets of paper. They were covered in calculations,

12

formulae, algebraic symbols and chemical terms.

'What did he do? Rush out in a frenzy?' I asked her.

'He changed into another man,' she said, calmly.

'Come now,' I said. 'You can't do that yet.'

'He did it.'

'How? By swallowing some chemical compound?'

'That, or electric transformations.'

There came another electric transformation in the shape of a blinding glare of lightning at the windows and a terrifying roar of thunder. When my eyes cleared of the coloured blotches left by the lightning I saw the lights had gone again.

I was about to snap my torch on when I saw a glass coil glowing with a flickering orange blue light.

'What's that?' I said.

'I don't know. It has not done that before that I have seen.'

'Have you seen it often?'

'I came in a week ago when he had gone. Then I came tonight to meet you.'

'The Steins wouldn't come back though they knew the doctor had gone?'

'They are frightened.'

'Of what? Why are they scared now he is gone?'

'They think he has left something here.'

'He certainly has, but what is there to be afraid of?'

The glowing coil seemed to brighten and there was a tiny whining sound from one of the tables. I went and shone the torch.

A small electric motor was running, though I saw no batteries and the house juice was off.

And then I saw something else. Beyond a heap of papers, tubes and wires there was a severed hand lying palm down on a small cleared space of the table.

Only it wasn't lying. The fingers were moving spasmodically as if trying to crawl along the table top.

The motor began to slow down and the fingers lost their horrible energy.

'What is it?' she said coming up behind me.

'Nothing,' I said and turned the light away from the table.

'I saw by your back. You were shocked. It was something there.'

Another flash and roar of the storm split up conversation. I let the light out for a moment. The glass coil was glowing again, and the whine of the motor started up once more.

I felt a sudden cold panic.

'Let us go downstairs,' I said and put the torch on again.

She went down ahead of me. I felt a bit surprised she did because she knew darned

14

well something had shocked me to the core.

When we got below again, I said, 'Is there any wine or anything about?'

'We will look in the kitchen,' she said, and led the way out.

We found some bottles in the larder and I poured some drink.

'What kind of visitors did he have, this doctor fellow?'

'Not many,' she said. 'But there was a man who came to see me and he came here. I did not see him after.'

'What sort of man?'

'A very angry sort of man,' she said. 'He was short with big hands–'

I shut my eyes a moment.

'Yes?'

'His hair cut short, clipped, fair. His name was Jodl, he said. He wished to see the doctor on urgent business!'

'Yet he didn't know where the doctor lived?'

She hesitated watching me.

'That is strange, is it not? I did not think of it before. If he was doing business with the doctor he should have known the address.'

'But he came to you first? How did he know that you were the agent here?'

'I do not know.'

'And after he came here, the doctor went away?'

'A day or two only.'

I took a long drink. I felt a horrible certainty that other pieces of Jodl were lying about round the house in unexpected places.

2

The lights came on. It would have been reassuring but for knowing that another lightning strike would blow them out again.

'Where will you stay?' she said.

'Not here,' I said.

'I will arrange for the inn to have you.'

She went and telephoned from an instrument at the foot of the stairs.

'Tomorrow I will make the Steins come and clean for you,' she said.

'Is it possible Frankenstein will come back?'

'His lease is finished. It finished two days after he had gone.'

'Oh. So he would have gone anyway?'

'Unless he wished to renew. I do not know whether he wished or not.'

At this point we heard a heavy engine thumping away outside the house. It stopped and she went to the window.

'It is a truck,' she said. 'Like a furniture truck. You did not order this?'

I shook my head. A hefty knocking at the

back door came and she answered it. A shaggy looking man appeared in the doorway. He looked rather like an ape with long hair and whiskers.

'Name of Frankenstein?' he said. His accent was American.

He had turned up in a quiet village in Germany but did not even try to speak German.

'Dr. Frankenstein has left,' Lilli said.

The caller pulled a dirty folded paper out of the breast pocket in his overalls.

'Got this order to collect chemical apparatus,' he said.

'Impossible,' I said.

'Do you mean he's bounced with it?' He looked from me to Lilli, then back again.

'No, it's here,' I said. 'But I have to hold it until I hear from him.'

'Property of the Company,' said the caller. 'Orders to collect.'

'What company?' I said.

'Continental Suppliers, registered Hamburg, parent company International Chemical Co., Detroit. Owner of the said property as listed.' He waved the paper.

'You can't take anything from this house,' I said.

'Property of the Company,' he said.

'I have no proof of that,' I said.

'Copy of the agreement,' he said, pulling another paper out of his breast pocket. 'Tex

17

Haynes, appointed collector unpaid accounts.'

'I'm sorry, Mr. Haynes. I also want to see Dr. Frankenstein. This is my house. At present I hold it and everything within for debt. My agent, Frau Braun has had the lawyers prepare the papers.'

Tex Haynes leant against the wall and regarded me.

'So, he owes you?' he said.

'Rent and damage,' I said. 'I have the legal right to hold everything on the premises until the Court decides otherwise. You must apply to them.'

'Courts take time, Buster,' he said. 'You don't know these Kraut set-ups. It's worse than back home.'

'What's the sum?' I said.

'Six hundred marks. You making an offer?'

'I don't want the stuff. I'm just holding it.'

I was on tricky ground for I didn't know the civil law but just guessed it was much the same as ours where proof of ownership was concerned. Lilli didn't complain, so I reckoned I wasn't doing too badly.

The thing was I didn't like Haynes, and though I felt sure he had the right papers, I wasn't going to let him start taking things out.

Nor did I want him to see that hand upstairs. I wanted to know a good deal more about the set-up myself before I let anyone start roaming about that house.

At the back of my mind was the idea that this Haynes man had come – not so much to collect chemical equipment as to collect the evidence of murder.

This was instinct, born of dislike for the caller and the stubborn feeling that the hand had been some mechanical contrivance and was no evidence of murder at all.

Haynes spun a chair to himself and sat down on it. He looked at us as he fumbled a squashed pack of cigarettes from his pocket.

'I didn't know you were invited,' I said.

'I'm a gate crasher,' he said.

'I'm a head crasher,' I said.

I got him by the shoulder and forearm as he put the cigarette into his mouth and threw him over the chair and out through the back door. It was a good toss even for one who practises judo pretty often.

The woman laughed suddenly.

Haynes picked himself up very slowly, then came back and leant on the doorpost.

'Invite me, then,' he said.

He pointed a gun at me. It was a sizeable looking automatic and he had the catch unsafe.

This action altered the whole aspect of the matter. I had my hand on the back of the chair since I had followed through on the toss.

It was just the question of a conjunction of

movements confusing the aimer. I swung the chair up and stepped back.

As I turned the chair he fired into the underside of the seat and the bullet didn't come through. By the time he should have fired again I crammed the legs of the chair right into his chest.

There was another shot but it hit the ceiling somewhere. He staggered back and I lifted the chair and bashed his head with it.

The stout Bavarian oak had resisted the bullet but it began to break on his head. He just went down there and lay on his back on the wet ground.

I saw the truck standing a short way off. Somebody got down from the cab and looked towards me. I got Haynes's pistol and fired to one side of the man's head. The shot hit the cab door at an angle, clanged and whined away into the trees.

The fellow also whined away into the trees, running like a sprinter.

I got Haynes and dragged him into the kitchen. Lilli watched quite calmly.

'Have you had anything of this sort before?' I said, slamming the back door shut.

'The man warned me there could be violence,' she said.

'What man?' I said.

'Jodl.'

'Go through and bolt the front door,' I said. 'And fix the windows.'

She went swiftly, quietly, quite coolly. I bent down and took the papers Haynes had put back in his pocket. They were carbons and could have been genuine or not. They repeated what he had said about firm's names and sites.

There was also a long list of items supplied with catalogue numbers alongside.

At the bottom of the list was typed, 'Cat. No. 0000 Human Hand price as quoted invoice 00000.'

Lilli came back. I put the papers on a table, folded.

'Thanks,' I said. 'You don't seem surprised?'

'This house is bad,' she said. 'The doctor turned it bad. One cannot be surprised now, whatever happens.'

She watched me as I had a look through Haynes's pockets generally.

'You seem to be used to it, also,' she said.

'No, it's just that the house is bad, one learns bad ways.'

Haynes carried a lot of money, a few assorted vehicle keys, comb, knife, chewing gum, cigarettes and a scrawled letter.

The letter said, 'Get F, 10,000 all details. Contact Beifeld 12 yes or no. J.'

The only reason why a man should carry a possibly incriminating letter when it could be remembered could only be that it contained a written suggestion that it was worth 10,000 whatever-they-weres.

'I have seen that man before,' Lilli said. 'He has been through the village. I am sure.'

'There's no name on the truck.'

As I said that the truck engine started and roared away. I ran through to the front room and saw the lights going out through the gates. They swung right and faded off altogether.

She came up behind me.

'I do not like that. They may fetch others.'

'Show me the house,' I said.

She did. It was a square block, four up, four down with conveniences worked in some time after the original building had been finished.

I kept thinking of the awful hand and the weird invoice for such a one. It occurred to me that it could be one of these imitation things budding doctors and surgeons try out things on.

Only I just couldn't believe it was.

It had been too real. Specially in the awful way the fingers had twitched and tried to crawl along.

The explanation seemed to me to be that a lightning charge had been picked up in force by the gasfilled coils, and this had radiated power out, causing the motor to work and the muscles of the hand to jerk by induction.

There was no difficulty about such an

explanation. It came by remembering the old galvanometer and the frog's leg muscles.

'You think that man is a crook?' she said.

'I think he came to get something the doctor had, but it wasn't repossession of hire purchase goods. You don't carry revolvers for that, nor do you get offered ten thousand of any kind of money when you get them.'

'But what did the doctor have, then?'

'What was the rumour that frightened the village people?'

'It was a story that he had changed himself into a werewolf by chemicals.'

'I'm a bit down on my horror film quizzes; what precisely is a werewolf?'

'A man who can change himself into a wolf.'

'When did this rumour start? Can you remember?'

'Not precisely. It has been gradually growing. I do not know for sure. One of the women coming by at night on her cycle saw a man, she thought, but when she got near it was like a man covered in hair and with teeth like a wolf.'

'Did it chase her?'

'She does not know. She rode madly and did not look back.'

I am not one of those who takes the common witness very seriously, particularly if the witness is badly scared at the time.

From these come men with glaring eyes and the rest of the nightmares. It can be very misleading. Ask a policeman.

'Might she not have mistaken this man here for a wild hairy beast? He has a lot of whiskers, you must admit.'

'This is a very reliable woman who speaks.'

I gave her another glass of wine and took one myself.

'Criminals do not pay large sums for devices to turn each other into animal shapes,' I said. 'Nor do spies. It does not seem to me to be a commercial proposition.'

'No. It is just to frighten,' she agreed.

'This doctor was here many years,' I said. 'Was there ever a rumour about him before?'

'Not that I ever heard.'

'What did they think he did here?'

'Study.'

'Then the rumour begins and the man Jodl came?'

'Yes. Oh yes, it was after the wild man chased the woman.'

He hadn't chased the woman. I detected a sense of alarm and uneasiness growing in calm, collected Lilli. I could not make out why it should begin now, when we had control of whatever the situation was.

At least we were locked in with Haynes's gun, which was two points up.

24

'So the shut away professor ceases to be a student and turns into a werewolf. Soon after, Jodl comes.'

'Yes–' She caught her breath a moment and half turned her head, listening. 'Yes. Like that.'

'Jodl comes here, we suppose and both he and Frankenstein disappear.'

She sat tense and did not reply for a moment.

'That is what happens, yes,' she said at last.

'This is over a week ago?'

'One cannot tell because no one knows when they went from here. When the lease was run out, I called but there was no reply.'

'And you called again?'

'I wrote. Then in two days I came again. There was no answer.'

'You tried the phone?'

'No one answered.'

She turned suddenly and looked out towards the stairs. She was taut and frightened then.

'Someone is upstairs!' she gasped.

We both kept still. Then I heard a sound up there, like someone tapping with their fingertips. I went dead cold.

'You stay here,' I said. 'I'll look.'

TWO

1

The chill on the back of my neck was acute and seemed to be crawling down my spine as I imagined what was making the noise upstairs.

I went to the door and looked up the stairs. It was dark up there but with something glowing from the open doorway of the lab. It glowed so that it shone obliquely on the black polished wood at the top of the stairs.

We both stood dead quiet there for a few seconds. A further tapping started up there. Cowardice was beaten by being frightened to look a coward. I went to the stairs.

The tapping stopped as I started to go up, so I stopped too and listened. All the time creaks and sighs, the normal noises of a house at night seemed to grow loud all round me.

The tapping started again. I went on up but when I got to the top it stopped. We had left all the doors of the rooms open and as I stood there I seemed to think the tapping had come, not from the laboratory, but from a room at the back of the house.

As I waited, it started again and this time there was no doubt it came from the room facing me then, at the back of the house.

I went in but did not use my light for a moment. There was a fair grey starlight through the many paned windows and I could see the empty bed. Then I saw a bulk of black shadow at the window.

I snapped the light on. It hit the many panes and splashed through on to a face of a sort I've never seen before. Distorted by the many panes it had a gross misshapen mouth, wide open, showing hundreds of teeth. Above that two glaring eyes, one higher than the other, gleamed under a brow of twisted hair.

For a moment I just stood still, shocked. The face seemed to fall back from the window. I ran, unlocked the latch and shoved the casements open.

There was nothing outside but trees dripping rain.

When I turned the light vertically downward I saw a hulk-shouldered figure climbing quickly down the wall. It reached the bottom and scuttled off into the trees where the beam of light became confused by the tree trunks and bushes.

That creature had not run like a man, nor shambled like an ape, but he had scuttled away like a great beetle.

I turned and ran back down the stairs. In

the kitchen Lilli was binding Haynes's head with a wet towel.

'It was someone outside,' I said.

She didn't say anything but just knelt on the floor and watched me fling open the back door. I ran out into the fringe of the woods where the intruder had gone.

It was a pretty hopeless search, for he had moved fast and a spotlight is no good when the beam is constantly split and blocked by trees and bushes.

I stopped and listened but heard only dripping rain hitting the ground.

Back in the kitchen I locked and bolted the door. Lilli was standing at the table then, smoking a cigarette. She watched me. Haynes was still out on the floor.

'I saw it through the distorted window,' I said. 'It didn't look like a man. It didn't move like a man when it ran off into the trees. Do you know anything about it?'

'It chased the woman. I told you that.'

It's one thing to disbelieve somebody else's story, it's another to try and disbelieve the evidence of your own sight.

The splitting vision of the many panes had made a horror of what could not have been a pretty face, but the strange movement of his flight had been queer indeed.

'The story goes, this is the doctor himself?' I said. 'Changed by some chemical experiment.'

'That is what they say. But it is impossible, also. One could easily compound chemicals that will grow much hair quickly, or atrophy the limbs so that they drag or make strange movements.'

'That is certainly so, I've no doubt but I can see no commercial benefits in working on such stuff.'

'You English always think businesswise. There is also the drive of curiosity, of wishing to know more, of wishing to try dangerous things.'

'Not with a name like Frankenstein,' I said. 'He picked that one.'

'It is not so unusual a name.'

'It is when you combine it with mucking around in forbidden science or chemistry or whatever it is. Do you know what?'

She watched me more intently than ever.

'Whenever I find strange things like this in a place,' I said, 'I always think it's something to do with crime of one sort or another. Of theft or smuggling, drug running – any of a hundred things.

'Even murder for money. That's a popular industry these days.'

'What have you seen to suggest such a thing in this house?' she said. 'All I see is a poor old man who works and has no more money left. That is why this man Haynes came here.'

'This man's a crook, you can take that

29

direct,' I said. 'I told you, debt collectors don't carry guns.'

She looked down at Haynes. His eyes were open but he stared at the ceiling as if wondering where in hell he was.

She was expressionless. Through the hour since I had met her she had kept, as nearly as possible in the circumstances, an enigmatic calm. It was almost as if she had not been surprised by the circumstances.

Even taking into account she had come full of yarns about wolf men and the wicked secret chemist upstairs, she should have been more emoted than she had been.

Haynes's eyes picked up some sharpening of intelligence. He sat up and looked at me from under the wet towel binding.

'Biefeld 12,' I said.

He looked puzzled a moment then shrugged.

'Okay. So what?' he said.

'Who's there when you get there?'

'A man.'

'What man?'

'A man who pays money. What other kind of man would I want to call?'

'I believe you. What does this guy pay money for? Chemical development?'

'What do you think I sell – aspirins?' He laughed scornfully and felt his head. 'Christ, you must have broken the chair.'

'I did. I'll break another one too. Any time.

Just call and collect – if you keep your mouth shut.'

He hauled himself up on a chair, then sat on it and leaned forward holding his head.

'Look, buster,' he said. 'I'm not in the talking business.'

'Not even for cash?'

'You don't know what you're bidding against, Mac,' he said. 'Forget it. Go back to peanuts.'

He sat back then as if feeling more comfortable. Then he grinned.

'Are you expecting somebody?' I said.

His eyes sharpened.

'You a mind reader?'

'No. I'm an old student of smalltime crooks.'

'Okay, yes. My buddy will fetch some relief.'

'From Beifeld?'

'From anywhere.'

'Let me put you in the picture,' I said. 'I'm big. I'm Beifeld 12. Your buddy comes to me and says you've balled it up and need help. I'm big. I'm Beifeld 12. I don't help mugs who get snapped up. I don't want mugs. You know what I do? I light a cigar and turn my back and get somebody better to do my work in future.'

Haynes swallowed.

'You're just a plain bastard,' he said.

'For sure. I'm Beifeld 12.' I sat on the

table. 'Well, I'll wait, and I'll bet you that stack in your pockets nobody comes for you by dawn. On?'

'I only back certs, Mac. I wouldn't cheat.'

'The bet's on anyway,' I said. 'You can't get out. So at dawn when it's all quiet and the birds are singing out there I'll take your wad.'

He fumbled for his cigarettes. When he got the packet out he stopped and looked, at them as if thinking.

'What's your line?' he said, looking up keenly. 'You don't talk like the innocent bystander.'

'I'm not. I'm an interested party.'

He put a hand to his head.

'I didn't know anybody else was in the field,' he said. 'It was supposed to be sealed off, this dump.'

'No seal is perfect. Listen, brother. You know what this is worth. Don't you think I'll be as tough as Beifeld 12 to get what I want?'

He was obviously thinking now and thinking hard. He was a mercenary, a purchasable conscience, a bought gun hand. Such men weathercock as opportunity blows.

He tossed the cigarettes in his hand.

'You offering business?' he said, looking up again.

'I'm not in the position where I have to make an offer,' I said.

32

I wanted him to blow what was behind all this, but he just sat there. Clearly my pretence had thumbed him right down, so far down that he was thinking of changing sides.

But he didn't talk.

I noticed Lilli was watching me with a slow ghost of a smile as if she knew a bit more of the truth than I did.

There are two reasons why a man won't talk. One, that he is under pressure; too frightened or too well paid to talk. Two, that he doesn't know anything to talk about.

The dim possibility that Two was the answer in Haynes's case came to me and I felt sad.

At this point of mutual thought we heard the tapping upstairs again. All three of us looked up to the ceiling.

It was the same sound. I thought it would be from the same source and ran to the back door.

I had it open and ran out, shone my torch, snatched from the table during the exit, pointing upwards.

It was there again, hanging on the window, it seemed. As the light struck it, it started and then swarmed right up and over the eaves out of my sight.

A human spider.

I ran outwards from the house trying to make the light shine up the steep slope of the roof. I backed into a wet bush and stopped. The light then sprayed the curly tiles of the roof.

No one, nothing was up there.

A woman screamed. The lighted window of the kitchen blacked out and there was a wild call.

'Come back!'

It meant me. Lilli was shaken at last.

I kept the light on the back door as I ran to the house, to make sure Haynes didn't run out. He didn't. When I got into the kitchen I found Lilli crawling on the floor, her hair torn into a wild wig hanging over her face.

Nobody else was there with her. I shone the light over her right through the hall, through the open door of the main room and to the still bolted rear door. Then I pulled her to her feet.

'He attacked me – ran upstairs–' she gasped. 'The wet towel – like a bludgeon–' She gave up talk, held her bosom and tried to stop its heaving.

She held her breath a moment in her effort to be calm. The whole house was silent.

I locked and bolted the back door.

'Watch it,' I said.

'Smashed the light,' she panted.

My torch showed the innards of the ceiling bulb hanging down from a fringe of broken

34

glass. My shoe grunted on broken pieces lying on the floor.

'Sure he went upstairs?' I said.

She nodded.

I went out and up the stairs, slowly, watching. I didn't want any dives on to my back from above. But there wasn't a sound up there.

It was dead quiet.

Dead was indeed the word.

2

The bedroom where I had first seen the spider man was the first call, but it was empty. I went through each room, very carefully, the bathroom, even the cupboards.

All this time there was no other sound but of me, and I was deliberately saving on decibels.

At last, and with a reluctance that makes the bowels twist a bit, I went into the laboratory.

Haynes was lying there on his back on the floor looking very unpleasant because he had been strangled.

I shone the light round the silent place. The shadows of the tubes and coils moved slowly round the walls as the light turned, but those shadows were the only moving things.

I straightened up and turned to the door.

Strangled.

Turning back for a closer look, which I didn't want to do, I saw the marks on his throat.

There were five marks, one on one side of the windpipe and the rest on the other.

A single-handed strangler.

Panicky that the whole thing was getting out of normality altogether I straightened and shone the torch over to where I had seen the hand.

It wasn't there.

The full force of Bavarian folk tales got me by the throat and I backed out of the room, slammed and locked the door.

I kept the light shining all round me as I ran down the stairs to the phone. Lilli was standing there looking up, her face white.

'Police!' I shouted. 'Telephone quick!'

I saw her pick the instrument off the hooks and then pull it right away. My light showed the cord was wrenched out of the wall.

She looked completely nonplussed by finding the cord broken.

'What the hell now?' I said. 'We'll have to get out of this place and fetch them personally. That man's been strangled up there.'

She dropped the phone to the floor.

'I'm not going from here!' she cried out desperately. 'It is sure death tonight. I will not go!'

'But I can't leave you here!' I shouted at her.

By this time I was rattled as a pea in a whistle and her reserve had quite gone.

'I will not go!' she said hysterically. 'I will not go!'

This was the moment for recrimination. I should have called the police when Haynes first showed what he was instead of waiting to find out what he was really up to and what my recent tenant had been up to.

I had relied too much on my home training to leave the police out of it. But at home there were things I cared about enough to want to keep them to myself. Here that caution didn't apply.

But then, I realised, Lilli hadn't run for the phone, either. She hadn't even suggested it.

'You rang the inn,' I said.

She looked sharp then, puffing her fallen tresses off her face to see me clearly.

'It was arranged, I told you. I telephoned, yes.'

Well, this phone was some relic from the backwoods that didn't have a dial. Anybody could lift the dingdong and start talking away without a soul being on the other end.

I think this was when I first felt dissatisfied with my agent.

She could have booked the room before she had come here, then played the phone game in my – not very close – hearing.

Only I couldn't think of any damn reason why she should.

One thing that did show up clearly was that she was frightened to a point near hysteria and in that state I wouldn't be able to persuade her to leave the house.

My idea was that if we talked a while it might ease her off to a point where she might decide to go.

I took her back to the kitchen and gave her a drink. She was very shaky.

'The lights do not come back,' she said.

'I think they've been cut off from outside.' I said. 'It's just an idea, but I think it's deliberate.'

But it didn't help to change her mind about leaving. She preferred to stay, even if in the dark.

'When did the Steins stop coming to clean up here?' I asked.

'It was when the woman saw the – the man. They did not come any more.'

'Did they think something was wrong here?'

'They were frightened.'

'But they had been working here for the doctor for a long time. They knew him well. Didn't they trust him any more?'

'He changed and then this monster came.'

I made a mental note that it had grown into a monster in her mind though she hadn't seen it, so she said. I had. If a monster

38

was anything humanly misshapen and abnormal then this was one.

But I still thought it was a man.

As I slowly drank some soothing wine I thought what I would like more than anything would be a large force of polizei surrounding the house and searchlights Illuminating the forest and the house and inside and all.

Perhaps if I got her somewhat stewed on the wine I could get her out without argument. It was a better proposition than trying to talk her out of it.

So I started being fairly light in tone of talk and kept refilling her glass. She took it like pouring it down a sink, with about as much result.

'We must get the police,' I said several times. 'The man's been murdered.'

'Then he does not matter any more,' she said.

'Don't you bother with murder here?' I snapped at her when I'd got fed with this answer.

'What is there to worry about? Somebody has murdered a criminal. It probably is another criminal. If rats eat rats you do not call the rodent officer. He is content at home.'

I kept looking out of the windows back and front to see if there was a sign of life anywhere. There was nothing until the lightning started up again. Then there was plenty, but it wasn't human.

The thunder roared and crashed, the rain hissed and the lightning drowned the torchlight time and again.

'Is it always like this?' I said during a lull.

'When the storms come they are always worse in the mountains,' she said, and poured herself another glass of wine.

The lull grew quite long and then I heard a tapping upstairs.

'Not again, for heaven's sake!' I said and turned to go up.

'I'll come,' she said, catching my arm. 'I do not want to be alone here.'

So instead of her getting easier about leaving it seemed the drink was making her determined not even to leave the room without an escort.

'Keep behind me,' I said angrily.

With the torch beaming ahead we went out and started up the stairs. But the sound was different from the old window tapping.

In fact it was a rapping on the landing floor above us.

'It is rain, coming in from the roof!' she whispered, and clutched my arm very tight.

'Does it usually leak?'

'No! But–' She caught her breath and did not go on.

'Come on! But what?'

I shook her and she eased a bit.

'There is a window in the roof up there. It

40

must be left open!'

'It wasn't open the last time it rained,' I said. 'You stay here.'

She stayed in the middle of the stairs and I went up and flashed the light in all directions quickly, in case anyone tried to dive out of the beam.

The rain was dripping regularly on the polished wood floor and coming down through a trap in the ceiling. The yellow wood door of the trap wasn't properly shut, so the rain was coming through.

The upper window must be open and the trap door wasn't put back right, so somebody must have been up there since the last storm and Haynes hadn't had time.

The spider man had been on the top of the roof.

I had a very odd feeling at the thought that he might have got in. Ugliness was beginning to make me feel the cold chills the villagers got over the wolfman.

In my mind's eye I kept seeing that gruesome distorted face through the panes, split, twisted, one eye up, one down, and I kept feeling he was coming up behind me, zipping along silently like a spider.

I was getting Them. It's very easy to get Them in the middle of a storm with no lights around and a murder already done.

But in a wild life I have come across chill makers before and I knew it was daft to let them get a hold.

After all, as Lilli had said, it was only a dead crook and perhaps he had been murdered by the orders of Beifeld 12.

Soberly thinking, I couldn't find any reason in the world why anybody in this area would want to murder *me*.

'What are you going to do?' she said.

'Fix the door.'

I got a chair and reached up, positioned the door correctly and bolted it with its two bolts.

'Somebody has got in,' she said. 'You will lock him in with us.'

I shone the light carefully in all the rooms and finally at the laboratory door. It was still bolted on the outside as I had done it.

'You have not looked in there!' she said.

'I locked it up. Nobody can bolt it from the inside.'

'You did not look!'

There was another roar and clatter from the mountains and the rain was pelting outside.

'I'll look if it makes you feel better.'

'Please look!'

So I went to the door, unbolted it and took the handle. Some small experience of being shot at makes me cautious about showing a light which tells where I am, so as I opened the door, I snapped the light off.

I put the torch round the edge of the door

and went to snap it on again when I saw another light glowing in the room.

It was the glass coil which had glowed redly before, but now it was brilliant orange and I could see a good deal of the room in the garish light.

It began to die and then another blaze of lightning flared at the windows and when it had died the orange light in the tube glared brightly.

I heard the electric motor whining faintly amidst the hissing of the rain outside.

It reminded me of that awful hand, and then of the one-handed strangulation. I shut the door again quickly and put the torch on.

'It is all right?' she said.

'Apart from the corpse, yes, perfectly normal.'

My voice ended up, drowned in a terrific clang and crack from overhead, a sound so violent that I thought the house had been struck. There was even that weird smell of sulphur you get when a house is struck.

A moment later I saw a line of brilliant light under the bottom edge of the lab door. It was so bright it showed up in the torch's beam even though it was a hair line from where I stood.

I put the light off again and watched the searing line of burning glow under the door. It was terrific. It looked as if the bottom of the door and the floorboards must start to

43

char under its fierce rays.

I opened the door. It was impossible to see into the room. It was so brilliant it seemed as if a sun had got trapped in it. I was blinded and pulled the door to.

'What is it?'

She called out urgently as I fumbled the bolts into their sockets again.

'Frankenstein's invention,' I said. 'Some kind of burning glass that works off lightning.'

'That is not possible.'

'It's perfectly possible to gather lightning. It depends what he wanted it for.'

Suddenly she hissed.

'My God! Someone is downstairs!'

I got her hand and heaved her up to the top of the stairs. Through the blotches of light colours in my retina I saw someone coming up the stairs towards us.

Very foolishly, I think now, I threw the torch at his head.

THREE

1

It showed the height to which nervous tension had jumped common sense, throwing a torch away like that.

But it hit him and went out.

I ran down the stairs and bumped him as he struggled to keep his balance on the stair. We closed, blind in the dark, and started pummelling and thumping in the hope of a wild knockout.

Lightning lit the scene as we lost our balance and went rolling and crashing down the stairs, mixed up together and still fighting. It was a stupid fight. All that could happen was that someone could be hurt by falling over something and breaking a leg or arm.

Lilli at the stairhead, didn't seem to do anything.

The man staggered to his feet, still holding me to find out which way to hit. I got up as well and hit out with a fine thump which, I think, must have hit him in the back judging from the feel. He hit a door and we fell through it together as it, unlatched, gave way

45

under our weight.

Once more we thumped to the floor, still fighting, hitting almost everything but each other. I got entangled with some chair legs and suddenly he sat on me but didn't seem to know it for he fell off again.

I got the chair off and then a swathe of brilliant light came through the darkness. It showed us both crouching but looking in different directions for each other.

As the light came we turned instinctively to continue the fight.

'Stop it!' Lilli cried from the doorway. 'It's the doctor!'

So we knelt there, breathing hard, and looked at each other.

'Dr. Frankenstein, I presume?' I said.

'One time,' he said. 'The name's Munt.'

We got up.

'It's been Frankenstein for years,' I said, remembering what had been told me by the solicitors.

'It had to be,' he said, peering at me. 'You are English?'

'I am your landlord.'

He made some sort of grimace, then got up and bowed his head.

'I am glad to make your acquaintance.'

'I heard that you'd gone,' I said.

He shrugged then.

'I had to come back. The storm, you understand. It is not so often that such a night–'

Another thump from the thunder shook the rafters. 'I wish to go to the laboratory,' he said, suddenly urgent. 'It is most important.'

'Before you go, it isn't quite as you left it,' I said.

'I can put it right, I think,' he said, and went out by Lilli.

We followed him up the stairs. He had a thin slack sort of figure, with great long legs that ate stairs four at a time.

He reached the lab door and was surprised to find it bolted. He was excited and fumbled the bolts but got it open and pushed the door wide.

There was a lot of that queer orange light in the big room then and a fair racket clattering in the sky.

Munt stopped on the threshold looking at the brightly glowing glass ring on the distant bench. The whining of the little motor could just be heard above the steady hissing of the rain outside.

I came up behind him.

'It is splendid!' he gasped, but he didn't think I heard.

He started forward to go into the room.

'Don't tread on the man,' I said.

He stopped, looked round over his shoulder, then ahead, then down to the floor. He stayed in the final position as if struck like it.

I came beside him and looked down. Haynes looked even worse than he had a little while ago.

'Do you know him?' I said.

'I have seen him,' Munt said. 'Yes. He belongs to a criminal organisation. He is better like that. Who killed him?'

'We don't know. He ran in here and was strangled. Strangled with one hand. Does that mean anything to you?'

'One hand? But he is such a strong man. Look!'

'Look at the marks.'

He looked. Then he hissed out breath and shook his head.

'It is not possible with one hand!'

'It has been done,' I said.

All this time I had been keeping a good look on the floor especially around the doorway.

'There was a hand here,' I said.

'A hand? What do you mean?'

His puzzlement seemed perfectly genuine so I told him what I meant. He looked round at me then.

'You joke. There is no such thing in my work. No limb–'

'It was itemised on your invoice which this man said he came to collect,' I said. 'One hand, it said. The list is probably still in his pocket now.'

'I don't understand!' he said.

'It was on the bench there,' I said, pointing. 'And when that light was on in the

48

coil tube the hand moved. It moved the fingers as if it tried to get along.'

'When was this?'

'I forget the time, but it was a period of storm activity, but not as heavy as this.'

He wiped his face with his hands. He was sweating. So was I. There was a lot of heat being generated in that place.

'They are using–' he began and stopped.

'Who?'

'I do not know. It is being twisted to witchcraft. Hand! I have never seen a hand like that! Where would such a thing be got?'

'After accidents. There's a lot of spare parts now. Hands, hearts, livers. You must have read about it.'

'It is horrible!' he said.

'Of course. Accidents are horrible. But the hand was here. Why, do you think?'

'To attempt an animation,' he said. 'I cannot think of anything else.'

'Is that what you were trying to do?'

'Good God! For what purpose would one try such a thing?' He turned on me in a rage. 'I am not that sort of a man!'

'You called yourself Frankenstein,' I said.

'I did not think of the connection at the time,' he said. 'I was pressed. Very much pressed. I had to think quickly. The name was on a film advertisement outside the phone booth. I said it. Once I had said it, I could not get rid of it. It was on my back.'

'Yet tonight you got rid of it,' said Lilli.

She had been behind all the time, calm, listening, but staying close.

'It matters no more,' Munt said. 'The reason for the masquerade is lost.'

'It was a stupid name to pick,' I said.

'When one is desperate one does not think of the consequences that come later.'

He went away, walking round Haynes without looking down at him, and reached the bench where the glass coil was. He began to lose himself in reading a lot of instruments there and began jotting things down furiously.

I went to him.

'One of us must get the police,' I said. 'We could not before because Miss Braun did not want to stay in the house alone.'

He did not hear, he was so engrossed. I said it again, taking his arm to underline the message.

He stared at me, without understanding.

Then suddenly he shouted.

'Der Polizei? Nien! Nien!'

He went on with a tumbling cascade of something that sounded to me like oaths with a few reasons in between. He was in some state about it.

When he calmed a bit I pointed across to the corpse.

'What do you propose to do, then?' I said. 'Here's a murder. A body.'

'I will get rid of that,' he said. 'He is a bad fellow.'

'That's nothing to do with it. This is a police matter and I want them here.'

'If you fetch them, they will find no body. This I promise.' He had very large long teeth and showed them in a bitter grin.

'But I am a law abiding man,' I said. 'I don't want to hide this murder and then be found out later and thrown into prison.'

'If you get them they will interrogate you, bully you, make you say things you would not, make you confess to what you did not do! You come from England where it is different, where they put murderers in cotton wool and let them out on parade. Everyone knows of this. But this is not so in Bavaria. Of this I assure you. You may ask Miss Braun. She will tell you that what I say is the truth.'

Lilli stood there looking at us and, carefully, at nothing on the floor.

'It is not so easy here,' she said. 'Now that the doctor is back, he perhaps knows what is best to be done.'

She had swung round to Munt. For the first time I remembered there was I in favour of calling the cops and being opposed by two who didn't. So often before it had been the other way about.

In my surprise over this I intercepted a look, a glance from Lilli to Munt and I realised then the reason.

There was something between them. And what was so surprising? They had known each other some years. They could have many common interests. They could be lovers, in which case I wouldn't stand much chance of opposing the combination.

But the situation was interesting, for Lilli had been quick to phone the police not long ago. Now she didn't want to call them.

Or had she tried to phone? Had she known the thing was pulled out by the roots?

This fitted with my earlier odd idea that she had faked the call to the inn.

And then an apparently obvious reason slotted in.

She didn't want the police because she thought Munt had done Haynes in.

So I changed the tracks rather unexpectedly.

'How did you get in the house just now?' I said to Munt.

He looked at me sharply.

'I have the keys,' he said.

'But the outer doors are bolted,' I said.

He stayed quite still and his eyes flicked to Lilli.

'Is there a secret way in?' I said. 'Or a hidden cellar which I haven't seen?'

He shrugged.

'There is a cellar,' he said. 'You are quite correct.'

It was fairly easy to be correct about such a thing as a secret hiding place known only to these two people. It followed the fact that the outer doors were bolted on the inside.

What was much more difficult was to make anything of the two people. A more blob-faced couple of blanks I didn't remember meeting. They seemed determined not to be anybody.

Outside, the storm seemed to have eased but there was a sudden blinding flash at the windows and an instant crash of thunder that sounded as if it wrecked the roof.

A second after it the orange light blazed out in such a glare of light that I threw myself to the floor to avoid what I thought would be an explosion.

And on the floor I looked along, and in the blotches of colour on my tortured sight I saw Haynes begin to move.

Lilli shouted. Munt gave some command which I didn't understand and I saw his long legs step right over me and go to Haynes.

2

The little motor was screaming and suddenly exploded in a blue flash and a lot of smoke. I noticed it purely as background. My attention was on Haynes's body jerking spasmodically as if making some ghastly attempt to get up.

Munt stood looking down at him. In the brilliant light from the glass coil he looked like the devil.

He also looked grimly delighted.

The light in the tube began to ease off. Haynes stopped moving. The galvanisation was over.

I should record here that throughout the demonstration following the lightning charge I felt electric pulses running through me as if a personal shocking coil had been applied to the palms of my hands.

The air was terrific then. Hot and tight with electric charge and with the smell of the burning motor it began to feel like the vestibule to you-know where.

I got up.

'What sort of research is this?' I said.

'Frog legs,' said Munt. 'You see him shake and jerk. It is just the electricity. A by-product of my work. A side effect.'

'What does it do that makes other people want it?' I said.

'It makes him work. You see that?'

'I saw it. It didn't look nice. I don't like these fairground tricks.'

I stood by the bench. Munt came quickly towards me, looking at something on the bench.

'You must not touch!' he said.

He grabbed at my wrist as my hand lay on

the bench. I snatched it up. He caught my wrist and seemed to shove it down again.

There was a crack that sent a bright light right through my mental world.

It was followed by a rapid sinking sensation and then a total blackness.

Every man is a fool at something.

How long the electrocution blackout was on I don't know. I wasn't much interested. When I came to all I was interested in was that I wasn't dead, that I had come alive again.

I felt my hands and legs and face to make sure the dream wasn't on. I looked up into their two faces. They looked as people must do to fish in a pond, blob-eyed, wet faced, gawping, stupid.

'I'm here,' I said.

Munt straightened up. His face seemed to shrink as if he had suddenly sailed up to a vast height above me.

I didn't get up right away. I laid there a while feeling somebody was playing a xylophone on certain lobes of my brain with knitting needles. But even with that I was glad to be alive.

Lilli was kneeling beside me and plastered my face with a wet towel. It seemed to be her cure for all. It made me feel better.

'You are all right,' she said.

'Fine,' I said, and got up.

It was not as easy as it sounds. I swooped

around a bit, clutching out at benches, then deciding not to touch and spinning on till I hit the wall with my back.

Where I ended up was by the door.

'You have had a shock,' Munt said from somewhere in the dizzy distance. 'Do not try too much for a little while.'

I felt I was trying to push the wall over, I stuck to it so tightly. The feeling I had was that if I relieved my pressure on the wall I could fall on my face ten thousand feet, without a stop.

'You will be better if you are calm,' Munt said.

Gradually I steadied up. I heard things, instead of feeling a ringing and roaring; I began to see things instead of them swooping past my vision like geometrical fly-aways. I could speak.

I said, 'Where's Haynes?'

And when I said that I seemed to recover altogether. The corpse wasn't on the floor any more. It wasn't anywhere that I could see.

'Where's Haynes?' I said again.

'He got up and walked away,' said Munt easily. 'You have a goddam pig that did it. Haynes was a pig, too.'

I was angry. Angry at being electrocuted, angry at being fooled. Munt had shoved my hand on that shocker and while I'd been out he'd got rid of the body.

So I went out and into every room and cupboard and downstairs and everywhere I knew and there was no Haynes.

'You've shoved him in your secret cellar!' I shouted up the stairs. 'Open it up. I want to see!'

'He is not anywhere any more,' Munt said from the top of the stairs. 'No recognisable part of him exists now. He has returned to chemical elements. He is better like that.'

'What did you do, tear him apart?' I shouted up.

'I disintegrated him,' Munt said quietly. 'After all, he was dead, was he not?'

What I know about scientific development is what can be read in the Sunday colour supplements. What's possible and what isn't is somebody else's business, not mine.

For all I knew he could have shivered the body into its original floating atoms and Haynes was now lying around the room as dust.

I didn't like that idea any more than I liked him lying there dead and ugly in a whole solid block. It was easier to think that he was hidden somewhere.

'Show me the cellar,' I said.

Munt shrugged, looked at Lilli, then came to the door. 'I will show you,' he said.

The storm had moved away somewhat, but from earlier performances over us I guessed it was making a circular track over the mountains and the village, going round and round.

I followed him down into the big main room. He backed up against my torch.

'Turn the light off,' he said tersely.

I did. We stood listening to the hiss of rain outside.

'What's the matter?' I said.

'I have a feeling–' he said.

'Of what?'

'At the windows,' he said briefly.

There were four windows looking out at the front of the house from that room, but they looked just faint grey squares in the general darkness.

And then a flickering glare of lightning lit up the trees and the drive outside. Rain on the roof of my car made a fuzz as it bounced up.

Beyond it, and against the trees I saw a number of figures standing, apparently facing the house.

Figures! It isn't quite the word for what we saw. In the lashing rain, the dying green glow of the lightning, and themselves fringed by a fuzz of rain, they looked like glass men standing, looking at the house.

'You see?' he said, his voice very low.

The lightning died and the thunder growled up in the mountains. Munt turned towards the stairs.

'Lilli!' he called.

58

He needn't have worried. Her dark shadow was on the stairs just behind us. She came up.

'He said they wouldn't come,' she breathed.

'Who? Haynes?' I said.

'Yes. He said they would. You were wrong about the big man. His troops have come after all.'

This was easy to believe. Possibly Munt believed it, too, though the sight we had seen didn't look anything of the normal sort at all.

Criminal forces, being spoilt boys mostly. Don't stand around in pouring rain just casing up the joint.

'We had best go down,' said Munt very quietly.

He went to the big table where I had first seen Lilli sitting and pushed the edge.

The whole black table began to turn over slowly on a pivot set in the floor.

'Sweeney Todd's chair!' I said. Anything for a laugh when things are black.

Another flare of lightning came. We all looked to the windows. The watchers were still standing there motionless, fringed with a spray of rain, blue lit, ghastly.

'They are nearer!' Lilli said. 'We must go quickly!'

'Shield the light and shine it here!' Munt said.

I got my hand over the lens and switched

on, pointing downwards. By the dim red-dish light we saw the long black slot in the floor under the table.

Lilli got down it quickly. Obviously she knew the way all right. Munt signalled me to follow.

There were a half-dozen steps down. I felt him push against my back as he came down very close after me.

The table groaned slightly as it rolled back into position above us. When the faint sound of movement stopped, Munt let out a breath of relief and snapped a switch.

Dim lights came on in what looked like a small room with a doorless opening on the left. More lights shone in there.

The first room had a number of crates of food, a sink in one corner and a lot of car batteries joined up in the other corner.

A place designed for a hidden man to live quite a while.

Lilli went on ahead through the opening into the other room. We followed her into a large room, very low but just high enough for me.

There was a good deal of furniture, so that one might live comfortably here. There was an opening on the far side matching the one we had come through.

The mouth of that was dark.

'All this was built during Hitler's time,' Munt said. 'It was necessary then for the opposition to have such tangible insurance.'

I was having a good look round but saw nothing of Haynes.

Munt went to a wall by a dresser and snapped a switch by a small grille. Nothing happened.

'From this one can hear what happens in the house,' said Munt. 'But it has had trouble which I did not repair. It did not work but spasmodically tonight. Once I heard you, but that was all.'

'How do you think those men will get in?' I said. 'The windows are too small the way they're broken up. A man couldn't get through for the mullions and bars. The main doors are locked and bolted on the inside. I noticed they are very stout.'

'They will get in,' said Lilli, standing rigidly as if trying to hear through the ceiling.

'How do you know?' I said, very curious now. 'Has this happened before?'

She looked at me very quickly, then up to the ceiling again.

'I think I heard something up there!' she whispered.

Munt tapped the instrument in the wall. There was a faint hearted crackle and that was all.

'Listen to me,' I said. 'I'm agog, you understand. This is my house but it seems that for years it has been a hiding-place for political stirrer-uppers. For that reason it has this convenient flat down here. What else is there? I want to know.'

'This is the only secret place,' Munt said. 'I know of no other – ah!' He turned to the grille in the wall. 'It is working!'

'I don't hear anything,' I said.

I went nearer and then heard a soft hissing. A moment later there was a rumble and growl of thunder in the speaker, then the hissing of rain went on again.

The sound of the thunder brought back the weird sight of the glass men out in the storm. The thing was out of this world as a vision; the stillness of them, the odd transparency caused by the rain and blue light were all set dead right for a horror film.

But so was the hand. And the disappearance of Haynes with a one hand mark on his windpipe. It was all a horror story.

The most horrible part was that it gradually crowded in on my brain that many of these things had no explanation that I knew anything about.

Could Munt have disintegrated that body? With the clothes, money and all? Was that what the machine, which was agitated by the lightning, really did?

I am a down to earth character. I don't believe in things that can't be explained. I don't want to believe in them.

The reason is that things I can't explain frighten me.

FOUR

1

'They're in the house!'

Munt's words chilled. They chilled because I could hear nothing but the soft hiss of rain coming from the speaker in the wall.

Lilli stood quite still, head cocked. I went closer.

'How do you know?' I said.

'You hear a softness sound – a kind of frou-frou – very slow,' Munt said.

He moved his fingers to a certain rhythm, his eyes on mine as if trying hypnosis.

Then I heard it; a soft rustling. The only thing I can think of to describe it was a number of people walking on a polished floor in feather slippers.

Obviously the sound we heard was being picked up somewhere at floor level upstairs.

'Who are they? Why don't they talk?' I said.

The memory of the glass men standing still and silent out there in the stormlight made imagination all too easy. I thought of transparent, fibreglass men walking about up there, thick limbed, soft, clumsy as snowmen.

And so silent.

The soft movements continued unevenly, as if some moved across the room, others stood still, then started off unexpectedly.

'They are searching,' Munt said.

The soft click of a cupboard door seemed to prove him right.

Yet I had the feeling the doctor was going on more than sound.

The noises faded. The searchers had gone into other parts of the house where the mikes did not pick up their sounds.

I sat on the arm of a chair and lit a cigarette after the others had refused.

'What do you know about these men?' I said.

'Bitte?' Munt said, pretending ignorance.

'Either you've seen or heard of them,' I said.

'One hears so much in these parts,' Munt said. 'The old legends die hard. In fact, I sometimes think they do not die at all. Wolf men, witches, phantom riders in the mountains, the maidens in the lake who snare the boatmen. There is always some resurrection of these tales. Maybe in different forms now, but the old ideas are still there.'

'Where there is a fall in organised religious belief there is often a return to hellfire thinking,' I said. 'But here it is mainly Catholic.'

'Mainly leaves many free,' said Munt with

a twisted smile. 'Free to believe what they will.'

'Okay, but these men up there. What do you know of them?'

'They are the men the American promised would come,' the woman said quickly.

Too quickly, I thought.

'Do they always wear asbestos suits?' I said. 'They look like men going in to put out an aircraft fire after the crash–'

The simile struck me at the moment I said it, but Munt seemed to have it in mind already. His eyes sharpened very suddenly.

'You already thought of that?' I said.

He shook his head.

'No. I had not thought of firemen.'

'They don't propose to burn my house down, do they?' I said, rather sharply.

'Why should they do that?' the woman cut in.

Her cutting in was designed to save Munt. What it did do was convince me that my idea that they were lovers was as right as made no difference.

'I've a mind to go up and make sure,' I said, getting up. 'After all, it's my property.'

She moved fast then and got herself between me and the way out to the table.

'No!' she gasped. 'Do not do that! You will die!'

'Why do you think we came down here?' Munt said over my shoulder. 'We are not playing a hiding game. But if we live for another day we may be able to fight again.'

'You do appreciate that I don't know what you're talking about?' I said. 'Why should anyone want to kill you or me?'

'To make sure that a man does not speak there is only one way,' the woman said.

'Speak?' I said. 'What in hell do I know to speak about?'

'You saw the American. You know he has gone,' she said.

'That was a straightforward case of murder – by some means,' I added the last words because I still could not get the ghastly hand out of my mind. 'And then you hid him somewhere.'

I turned then and took Munt by surprise. He was wiping a hand round his wet face. He looked as if he were more frightened of me than of the incredible intruders up in the house.

'That is not the case. I told you–' he said, and stopped it seemed for want of breath.

'You keep saying you atomised him,' I said. 'I've never heard of anyone doing that, and I don't believe you can do it either. You deliberately put me out and while I was out you hid that body.'

'It does not exist any more. You must believe me,' Munt said.

We said no more then. The frou-frou sound came back into the speaker. We heard it shifting about the big room over our heads, though we heard nothing directly.

There was still no sound of talk or whispering, no communication at all.

Then the sounds of movement faded, and ended with a very soft thump, like a door shutting. A silence followed. Even the hissing of the rain had stopped.

Then there was a sound, a rich sort of shiffing sound followed by a 'chuck'.

'Somebody is bolting the door,' Munt said and wiped his face again. 'So they have gone.'

He looked at the woman. She nodded. I looked from one to the other.

'Gone?' I said. 'But that was the sound of the door being bolted. The bolts are on the inside! Whoever did that is inside still!'

Munt shook his head slowly.

'You will learn that normal physics do not matter to these things,' he said. 'Bolts, iron bars – none form a barrier to them. It is as if the iron dissolves.'

'This is about the biggest load of cock and bull I have yet come across,' I said. 'Do you mean they are ghosts who reach through solid doors as if they didn't exist?'

'That is what they do,' the woman said.

'So they reach through a solid panel as if it wasn't there,' I said, 'yet can get hold of a solid bolt on the other side. There's something illogical, isn't there?'

Again man and woman looked at each other, as if they hadn't thought of that one.

'But they do it,' she said, stiffly.

'I wish you'd tell me what you know about these people,' I said. 'I hate being left out.'

We listened again for a whine but there wasn't a sound from the speaker, just an occasional crackle from a loose connection somewhere.

'There is no one left,' Munt said.

'Let's go up and try,' I said.

Again an exchange of glances.

'Well, you said it was safe,' I pointed out. 'I didn't.'

Munt nodded. We went back through the outer room and up the steps underneath the table. He turned the lights out.

In the darkness I heard the very faint heavy sound of the table rolling over on its bearings. It stopped.

After a moment I could see the grey light from a window reflecting in plates on an old dresser against the wall.

There wasn't a sound anywhere.

Munt clambered out into the room and I followed him. I looked first towards the windows. The grey light outside seemed to be the first streaks of dawn filtering up over the mountains.

The night had taken longer than I had realised.

Except I hadn't counted for the time I had

known nothing about it.

As I smelt the first fresh tingle of new air after the storm and brightening with the dawn, I began to feel more myself.

It was about then I realised I hadn't been behaving like myself. I should have kicked up hell's own row over that knockout trick, but after it I seemed to have been dull and confused, unable to get things sorted out.

We used the torch again to look round the house. Snapping switches still showed the main juice was off. Nothing seemed to have been moved, but then, the place had been in such a mess before it was really difficult to be sure.

Upstairs the bedrooms were as before. The door to the laboratory was open.

Again I thought of that awful hand.

The glass ring no longer glowed. The grey light from the windows showed everything to seem to be much as before.

Munt didn't take the same view though he said nothing. He walked quickly about, from bench to bench, picking something up, putting it down, going across to another bit of apparatus and looking at that.

Lilli rapped out some questions in German.

'English, please,' I said.

Both looked at me.

'I asked if they had touched anything,' she said.

'They've touched everything,' Munt said. 'Everything is displaced.'

He waved his hands about, indicating the whole room.

'Have they stolen anything?' I said.

He shook his head then and stared towards the sarcophagus in the corner.

This house was in many ways original and in all the bedrooms was one of these German room heaters. They are big terracotta cupboard-like things which stand in the corner. They are about seven feet high, three wide, three deep with an oven in the middle. The oven is closed and filled with smouldering sawdust. Air goes into the sarcophagus at the bottom, rises up round the fire and issues forth from an unseen grille at the top, all hot.

These heaters, with their heavily ornamented and colourful finishes went through a phase of being muck heap fodder and are now valuable again.

What brought my attention to this one was that Munt looked quickly over at it, then turned his back.

'Nothing is stolen that I see,' he said. 'Nothing material, that is. But undoubtedly they have stolen my brains!'

'Could anyone with scientific knowledge recognise what you were working on here?' I said.

'The actual figures are not there. I do not write such things.'

'They could get on without them?'

'If the road is pointed out to one, the way is not so difficult.'

Again I saw his eyes flick across to the old heater. I began to get an idea where Haynes might be hidden. Especially if the old oven part of the monster had been taken out.

'It is very late,' Lilli said. 'What shall we do now?'

'I'm going to lie on a bed here,' I said. 'I can't turn up at the pub at this time in the morning.'

'I can get some food,' she said.

'Do as you wish,' I said. 'I'll rest a while.'

I needed a rest. I needed to think.

I went into the main bedroom, slung off my jacket and laid down on it, staring up.

And while doing that I saw a huge moth hanging on to the top of the curtain on the left of the window.

Only as I looked harder I saw it was not a moth.

It was a hand.

2

I remember I yelled and flung myself off the bed. The others came out on to the landing from the lab and called out in German.

'That bloody horror's in here,' I said, going to the door. 'Munt! Come and look.'

71

He came, passed me and walked into the room looking up to where I pointed. The woman stayed out on the landing.

'Is this the – thing you talked about?' Munt said, staring up.

'I hope there aren't two,' I said.

He shone the torch up to get a better look. I didn't bother to look.

'It is fixed there with the loose cotton loops on the curtain,' Munt said. 'This is interesting.'

He snapped the light off. His tone was odd indeed, like that of a man who remembers something of great importance which soothes his cares almost away.

'Make it interesting for me, too,' I said.

He sat on the end of the bed.

'The sense of humour is reminiscent.'

'If you call this humour, you must have some twisted variety yourself,' I said.

'It is a kind of thing that one man would think funny,' said Munt. 'It would be funny to him because he would know it would make everybody else sick with horror. That kind of fun.'

'All right. Who is he?'

'He has practised surgery but was stopped because nobody knew where he had studied, or where he had practised to begin with. It was thought that perhaps he learnt his trade practising in the Camps – of which you may have heard. Many experiments.

Very foul.

'But some years ago he disappeared and it seemed that after a while he did well in England, but it was not in surgery. Some kind of experimenting, physics perhaps. But he went wrong there, also, and it is thought he was dead.

'But this–' he pointed to the curtain, '–brings back only the one man.'

'What was his name?'

'You are very keen to bring things to earth, Herr Blake,' Munt said. 'This will seem like floating. I know of a half-dozen names, none very helpful. Braun, Schmidt, Wurms, Gallaud, Bauer, Bonnsteine, Stumm– These I have heard of he uses. There may be many others.'

The only one that lit up to me was Bauer. For a moment I didn't quite remember why, and then I connected it with *Lohm.*

Lohm is an industrial espionage group, friends of mine, who once had dealings with a Bauer who was attempting to put human brains into computers. This sort of thing might work someday, but apart from its sickening idea, it isn't yet allowed.

Now as I recalled *Lohm* I seemed to remember also that Bauer had been presumed dead in an explosion at his workshop.

The thing about explosions is that you can never be really sure what went up and what didn't. Some have crawled out of what looked like supreme devastation quite unscathed.

And again, when semi-scientists wish to disappear nothing could be easier than to arrange an explosion from which he thoughtfully removes himself first.

Further, owing to the peculiar nature of Bauer's work there were a number of human spare parts lying about that place at the time of the bang, so that it might have been rather hard to decide which bit was whose.

I remember the *Lohm* people holding out at length on that case because it was their only experience of having seen a charnel housekeeper appointed by a large firm on the supposition that he was something quite other.

It was an interesting coincidence, something a bit more than one name amongst seven. The man indicated was one who was used to chopping off hands and using them to scare people. Not as a medical student's hoax either.

I said nothing of this to Munt but went to rest on a bed in another room.

For a while I slept, more from exhaustion than anything. But towards the time I woke up I had some pretty glorious nightmares. Walpurgis Night specials.

When I woke up the dreams faded and even the events of the previous night looked normal colour.

Except Haynes was dead somewhere. That still bothered me, but as he had been part of the hand trick I didn't care so much.

It was dead quiet in the house then. Out on the landing I couldn't hear a thing. The laboratory door was open. Like a small boy I felt a twinge of guilt or fear at being found out as I went towards it.

The room seemed the same mess as on the previous night, but the layman couldn't be sure. There was so much stuff about.

And most of it owed for. This thought struck me and brought back the invoice, because I was going to look for Haynes anyway, so the link wasn't obscure.

I went up to the old heater and put my hand on its shining ceramic surface. It was warm. It was very warm, and as it was summer and hot enough anyway, the warmth was odd.

I opened the door of the firebox. Instead of a firebox there was some kind of bolted metal wall inside with a closed opening, rather like a manhole on a big boiler, with a very powerful locking bar. The metal was bluish.

This was no room heater. It had been adapted to some kind of a chemical or electric furnace.

Connecting Munt's glances with this contraption, I thought of the disappearing body. In an oven like this it would probably be simple. You shoved it through the manhole, closed up, set things going and soon there would be a lot of ash and calcined bones.

Very hygenic, come to think.

It answered the question which had been bothering me and cleared the way for all the other things which were bothering me.

It was now full daylight and possible to go in and call the police. But obviously if I did, Munt would be taken in, and I didn't feel I wanted him in yet.

In the first place I didn't think he had killed Haynes, and in the second I was sure he was hiding from characters far worse than he was.

The mention of Bauer had fired my rude imagination. I kept thinking of what the *Lohm* bods had said about him, and about Beifeld 12.

The mess downstairs was as before. Nothing seemed to have been done. There was no sign of anybody in the house with me. I went to the rolling table and put a hand on it, but decided not to tip it.

In the kitchen I drank some water and got an electric kettle. Then I went and tried the light in the hall. It didn't come on, so I gave up the kettle gambit, got some bread and cold ham and had that with cold water for breakfast.

Nobody came.

I didn't try the phone because the line was still hanging down the wall with a fuzzy end.

It was a funny feeling, being alone in the dead quiet of the place by daylight. It would have been better at night.

The house showed up as rather faded and in need of a respray. Quite apart from the untidy mess it was in it clearly had had nothing done for a very long time.

I went outside and had a look at the forest. The trees rolled right up the grand slope of mountains to right and left. There was a lawn at the back which resembled a hayfield and a summerhouse beyond a small pond with its back to the trees.

As I looked at it I suddenly thought I saw a face behind one of the dirty paned windows. It might have been the sun catching the pane for an instant, but the face seemed to me to draw back.

I went along a path to the summerhouse, not hurrying in case somebody watched.

The summerhouse was a pleasant wooden building with three rooms. Nothing was locked.

No one was there.

A fair amount of furniture was around, as if the place was used to live and work in during hot weather. It was as untidy as the house but looked as if it had been in very recent use.

There were a number of sheets of paper scattered on a table by the veranda door, some scribbled on, others containing a mass of those algebraic wonders, all brackets and cube root signs. Munt's, I thought.

I shuffled the papers, spreading them so I could see if any one carried a signal I could understand.

There was one.

It was a plain sheet, but written across the middle in a thick black felt pen was a message.

'Keep away from Beifeld 12 and see Bavaria in comfort.'

A lengthy message for its kind, and in English. But it couldn't have been Haynes. The block letters were plain, Anglo-Saxon type, no curls, no frills such as one finds in the Continental hand.

Haynes had been speaking about Beifeld with confidence, so even if it had been done before he died, he would have saved labour just by telling me.

In fact, in a roundabout way, he had said just this.

But whoever wrote the message had heard what Haynes had said to me, because in the short time I had been here, he was the only one who could have told me.

If Munt had known about Beifeld, he would have gone there himself.

I had a good look round the wooden

building, especially under the tables, but I needn't have worried to look for secret passages as a getaway space for the face I had seen.

Behind a big wall map was a back door. I held the map aside and looked out into the forest. The birds were making a fine din. It was a lovely morning to be alive.

I had a good look at the wall map round the area of the house but couldn't find a Beifeld.

Back in the house I looked up the telephone book. There were Beifeld numbers but no double ones. They were all four figures, even to the point of putting noughts in front to make up.

So there wouldn't be a Beifeld 12, but Beifeld 0012. It's something to do with the mechanics of the exchange organisation, STD or something.

So there was no Beifeld on the map, yet there was one in the local telephone book and general guide. So it was just the name of an exchange.

And there was no 12.

The place to clear some of this confusion was the local Post Office. At least they would know whereabouts the exchange was.

I went out the front to my car and looked around. The birds were tremendously in song. But I was alone with them.

Back in the house I looked at the long

table and at last tipped it. It tilted very easily and almost in silence, a beautiful job.

It was dark below. None of the battery lighting system was in operation. I called. My voice echoed back. Nothing else came.

I rolled the table back into position and looked round the room. I could almost feel the tenseness it must've lived through when the storm troopers were after the unlucky inmate. The Nazis didn't just persecute Jews; they flayed all dissenters regardless.

I wondered what kind of men had hidden here, talking quietly, the strained, listening pauses between each sentence.

And then I wondered who had had the house then. My grandfather had been dead a few years; in fact he died not long after Hitler came in.

The tenant couldn't have been Munt then. Munt wasn't old enough. Besides there was that story about him catching the name Frankenstein from a poster outside a phone booth.

This must have been when he had fixed the tenancy.

With Lilli.

She couldn't have asked many questions, I thought, when I realised this. A man thinking of this name in a moment over a phone, and the agent asking no references, not even checking on his name, was an impossible idea.

Unless they were lovers before the tenancy. She wouldn't have asked any questions then.

And now they seemed to have sloped off together. Had they run? Had they decided that the house was no longer safe, even with its hideout?

That, too, I might get an idea of, down in the village.

FIVE

1

The village was all in the trees, old-fashioned, deliberately decorative, a tourist draw. This spelt good for me because it meant my single language effort wouldn't be a drawback.

So I went to fill up at the garage. A bald fat man came out smoking a cigar and beamed like a happy cheese. He spent a little while pointing out the qualities of his various juices, then stuck the hose into my tank and let it go on while we talked.

He asked if I was touring and all the usual questions, and I answered everything as openly as I could.

Then I said, 'I'm not only touring. I came to see my house here. Karen.'

He took the thick cigar from his mouth, cocked his head and his eyes almost disappeared in bags of cheese.

'So?' he said. 'Der Englander at last?'

'Have you been waiting long?'

'It cannot be the same,' he said. 'The last time was I was a small boy, perhaps ten, and he was a big straight old man with a chaffeur and we always wonder why he have the chaffeur because he always drive himself. I think he was what you call a butler.'

'Did he come often?'

'He came now and again. Very rich. All the children were frightened of him because he was so stern, so fierce, but when they got to know they would go up to Karen and he would feed them with Frau Gilderstein's cakes and tell them funny stories.

'One day I was there and I heard him speak with the chaffeur and he say, "Take the children away now, Benkin, I want to get drunk".'

He laughed and the tears squeezed out of his eye pouches.

'He died a long time ago,' I said.

'After he die nobody come from the family,' he said, and shook his head.

'Who took the place then?'

'For a long time there was nobody. Frau Gilderstein look after it, but nobody come. Then she die and we think somebody must come now from England, but nobody come.

'Den dere is a lot of war talk and the Army come and take it, I think because it is owned by the English, and this make them laugh. They keep it all the war, I hear, but I do not see for I am away in the war myself.

'Then some American army take it over and stay a little bit, and then I come home from England. I was in camp there, you know, four years, more. I was prisonered from Rommel in the desert, you know? So I get to South Africa and then back to England and learn to make toys and so I come home.'

'This is a long time ago,' I said. 'Who has been in the house since?'

'It stood alone a long time, but the agent always saw it was kept clean and painted. Then a man had it for a holiday house, you know, and we see him in the hunting time only.

'Then suddenly the doctor is there. It is some time ago now, and always a pleasant man, you say. But lately–' He shrugged and looked askance.

'What happened to him lately?' I said.

'There are many tales. People are like that. If you do not know you make it up. For myself I would not say, but suddenly you see him no more, yet he is still there.'

'He has gone,' I said. 'His term of tenancy ended a few days ago.'

'I did not know that. Some will be sorry.'

'Moneywise?'

'It is no business of mine. I am glad to see you. I hope you will be happy visiting us. Or will you live for good?'

'I'm not sure yet. At present, call it a holiday.'

'I am so glad.'

'Do you know a telephone exchange called Beifeld?'

'Beifeld?' He rubbed his bald head and smoked slowly. 'Oh!' He laughed. 'It is only a box in the forest, that. All automatics, you know.'

'But not here, I notice.'

'Oh, no, we still have Frau Benz. I do not know what she will do when she can no more hear what everybody in the village says.' He laughed again.

'And the Steins,' I said. 'They looked after my house?'

'Ah! And they will not go again suddenly. I think they make up a story about it, but it frighten them, too. They go no more, suddenly.'

'Where do I find them?'

'There is a little shop. You go down the village and on the right hand, a little shop. She sells my toys and the tourists go home and say what wonderful Bavarian workmanship, though they taught me in England!'

He laughed again.

I said I would go down and find them but he insisted on a routine check on tyres, water, oil, battery, cleaning the windscreen, filling the washer bottle.

It took a long time.

He told me how to get to Beifeld, but having heard it was one of those small brick boxes full of clicks my interest began to wane.

I couldn't imagine a full time crook with grandiose ideas of drama calling himself after one of those.

But I had forgotten the 12.

He finished at last and I paid him with a guilty feeling it should have been twice as much with all the trouble he had taken.

I could have walked down the road. It was a small fairy tale village and the Steins' shop was like the rest, all small panes and bottle glass, steep pitched roof, black and white wood, every bit a carver's whimsy.

The shop was full of wooden toys and ornaments. It was a world of wood, and very beautifully handled wood, also.

I had a good look round the stuff and there was everything to show the skills of the artful carver down to the whimsical whittler. I love clever woodwork.

A stout grey-haired woman came in from somewhere at the back. I told her who I was.

'Oh. Ah. Ja. You come in, please. Cake and coffee. It is just time.'

So I went in and had cake and coffee in a room overlooking a lake. It was broad and smooth and lined with inevitable trees. Here and there buildings like cakes themselves peered out of the green towards the water.

'Why did you leave Mr. Mun – Frankenstein,' I said.

'Bitte?' She stalled.

'What made you go suddenly after so long?'

She twisted her hands about. I got the impression she had been, and still was, genuinely worried about Munt's development.

'He experiments with things,' she said. 'One never knows.'

'But he was experimenting all the time you were there, wasn't he?'

'Yes, but somehow it was not the same. I do not know how to say. Something changed.'

'In his work or in his manner?'

'The manner, yes. Always he was very nice gentleman. Very pleasant, friendly. Very easy, you say, he do not mind what you do so long as the place is nice.

'So when my sister died and I have to take the shop he say that is all right, you arrange it all to suit yourself.'

'Your husband was there as well?'

'He do the garden and carry heavy things. He is only there but a few hours in the week, that is.'

'Now when Mr – the doctor changed, how was the change? What did he do that was different?'

'He stay in the laboratory all the time. If I try to go in and take him coffee or sandwich, or what, he keeps the door locked and shouts. Angry shouts.

'I say to my husband he is ill, but he does not look ill in the body. My husband say it is weltzschmerz he has got. The sickness of the world, so he try to think himself out of it before he go mad with blackness.'

'You thought he might be mad?'

'I do not know. He is so different. All of a sudden it is like this. He is shut up and locked in and angry all the time.'

'Did he have visitors?'

'He have a few, yes. But not after he change. He will see nobody then.'

'But before. Who were the visitors?'

'Always people from far off. From Munchen some, for I took up the cards.'

'Any Americans?'

'I do not think so.' She frowned out at the lake. 'There was an Englishman who come several times, very cheerful, jolly man. Always laugh and wink and make fun of the doctor working so hard.'

'Do you know his name?'

'A Mr Hardcastle, I think it is.'

My thinkpoint had shifted from the criminal possibilities to Karen itself. And I remembered the item which had brought it to my notice the suddenly increased annual expenditure on Karen.

Eight hundred and forty-nine pounds.

This was a very large sum to spend on maintenance, even including a complete redecoration of a house that size. And I had myself seen that morning that nothing had been done there for a few years.

Eight hundred and forty-nine is not a number that readily springs to the mind. It has to have a reason before it arrives at all. A sum of money spent, or a sum going to be spent to meet an estimate.

'Was the house to be redecorated ?' I said.

'We keep saying it must, but Miss Braun she keep saying not to disturb the doctor in his work. And so it is put off.'

'When was it last done?'

'Five – six years ago. Yes, I think.'

Now I reckoned that between them these part-timers got about three hundred a year and the other hundred was for local rates and such, although the tenant should have settled for them. I did not know German law regarding tenancies and the payment of local taxes. It was something I should have to track down.

This still left four hundred and forty-nine over the annual norm and there was evidence that this number of pounds had not been spent.

So what had it gone on? To pay some of the doctor's overdue chemical bills? Perhaps. Miss Braun could have swung such a trick and probably would, if needed.

Sitting there, looking at the sunny lake, Haynes seemed quite unreal. I kept trying to tell myself he had been murdered and cremated in a chemical furnace.

And as I realised it was probably the truth,

so I realised it was probably a good thing for the world at large.

The thought that it might also be a good thing for Beifeld 12 loomed now and again but I didn't like it enough to develop it.

'Do you know what the doctor was working on all this time?' I said.

'Natural forces, natural forces, he kept saying. He is always very excited when the storms come. They ring and tell the weather every morning from the weather station so that he can know what it will be.'

'Did he tell you anything about his work?'

'Sometimes he will come and hug me and dance around and be very happy because it goes so well.'

'Surely he said something at such times?'

'Sometimes he say about wars.'

'What about wars?'

'He says no more because the weapons will be kaput.'

'The weapons!'

'Ja. So we dance round and then he rush upstairs again and go to work and I hear him singing up there.'

'Because the door is open?'

'Ja. But not after. Not since the—'

And there she stopped and I saw her hands twist.

'Since the what?' I said.

'Since the wolf man,' she whispered.

2

That whisper had the effect of a piece of ice sliding down the knobs on my spine. After all, I had seen the joker scaling the walls and the roof and sidling around like a spider, and though I thought he must be a man, even if deformed, the memory was always a bit shaking. It still is.

But by that time, many hours after, I had slotted the wolf man into a logical column.

Somebody wanted the details of Munt's work. If that somebody knew, say a circus act, a hairy man who could climb like a fly or spider, that could be very useful to him.

Such a man could shin up, peer in upon the busy man, see what he was doing and slope off with the information.

At the same time, if he was seen – and he had been – he would stir up the old fears in the local public, who had wolf men in their fairy-tales from the year dot.

It was a primitive way of getting information, but all the new and sophisticated ways were being jammed and blocked by equally sophisticated defences. In such circumstances a man looking in the window was still a good method.

This boiled down to Munt being spied on.

If the reason for the spying was some kind of anti-weapon device, then this affair moved out of the realm of personal intrigue and into the espionage bracket.

In which case it was not a small matter of a peculiar tenant in my little German house but very big business indeed.

'The wolf man,' I said. 'Somebody reported him to the police?'

'Frau Grien was riding her bicycle and saw him. She reports but the police do not take much notice. You see, nobody was touched, or chased and they think she has seen a tramp. There used to be many such. Not many now, but still some.'

'Where did she see him?'

'It was close to Karen.'

'And then the doctor became different?'

'When next day we get there he is locked in and will not come out. So my husband says perhaps something has changed him.'

'Didn't you see him after that time?'

'No. He shout through the door. We stay two days and then come away.'

'And you thought that some experiment had changed him?'

She started to cry.

'It is certain!' she sobbed. 'He was so nice, but it is always dangerous to experiment with things one cannot be sure of. So many things go wrong. The wrong chemicals and there is terrible deformity. It is not rare.'

I let her sob it out.

'You haven't seen the doctor since?'

She shook her head.

There was a jangle of a bell from the shop.

'If you please, there is someone in the shop,' she said.

A man came into view at the end of the veranda, a thin tall fellow in trousers, shirt and open waistcoat.

'Is that Herr Stein?' I said, pointing.

'Ja. I will tell him.'

'You look after the shop. I'll introduce myself.'

I went out to Stein. He produced a curved pipe from his waistcoat and hung it in his teeth as he looked at me. I told him who I was. It seemed only to concentrate his gaze.

He took the pipe out.

'It is good you come,' he said, his voice very low in his chest. 'The police will do nothing. They think all wish to get rid of the doctor and make up stories.'

'You have seen them?'

'They came to see me. I do not like them over much. I was once questioned by the Gestapo and I still have the marks.'

'These are different police.'

'They are all police,' he said.

He was clearly a man not easily persuaded against his opinions.

'What did they ask you about Frankenstein?'

'They think the whole damn thing a joke, because of the name people imagine monsters and the rest of it.'

'You speak English very well.'

'It is compulsory at school, and since the war most visitors speak English. There is good practice.'

'But they didn't imagine monsters until the wolf man?'

'They think of these scientists as like on the movies,' he said with a faint sneer. 'They learn everything from the movies and the television.'

'What sort of man is the doctor?'

'I see him not much. I do the garden and carrying and I see him only when he is writing, out in the summerhouse. He is always frowning, writing something. When he wants something he barks like a dog for me to tell Marthe. He is a sour man.'

Or perhaps sour Stein didn't get on with Munt.

'Did you notice him change?' I said.

He hesitated on that one and fiddled with his pipe.

'She says so. I would not know to make up my mind.'

'She means he used some chemical and turned himself into a wolf man.'

He shrugged.

'She is like the others. All movies.'

'You don't think it's possible?'

'Very wonderful things are done, but–' he shrugged again, '–no, I don't think it possible. After all, it is easy to get beards and whisker and put them on the face.'

'You know the table in the dining-room?'

He flicked a glance at me, then looked down at his pipe again.

'I do not go in the house much. That is Marthe's.'

'But you know it?'

'Of course.'

'It is fixed to the floor,' I said.

'It is heavy,' he said.

'Is it? I felt as if it was fixed when I tried it.'

'Very heavy,' he said.

'Did you run errands for the doctor?'

'Ja.'

'Tell me about them.'

'I go into Schwarndorf to fetch things for him. Things for his experiments. Sometimes they do not want to give over to me, because of the bills, but it is not my affair. I do what I am asked. That is all.'

'You saw some visitors he had?'

'Oh – not many. I am there only for the garden and carrying. I am a carpenter but have not much to do now all the things come ready made from the wood factories.'

'But you saw some?'

'Now and then I see them.' He laughed suddenly. 'There was one and the doctor was in the summerhouse. Ja. I remember that. But a man, like a hippopotamus and

95

hair like spikes all stick out all round. Well, they start to shout and bawl and roar and bark and there is a fight.'

'You didn't go to help?' I said.

'I move carefully,' said Stein, touching his shoulder. 'I get rheumatism very easily, then I cannot work at all.'

'What happened with the fight?'

'The hippopotamus man come away with blood on his face and get in his car and away, cursing like mad.'

'What was so funny?'

'Because he come as a man to sell the doctor something. I never saw a salesman like that.'

'Do you remember his name?'

'Yes, I remember he said it was Beifeld, but I don't know what it really was.'

I began to get excited inside but kept calm outwardly.

'How long ago was this?'

'Not long before. About three days. There were no visitors after.'

'Will you come back when I need you?' I said.

'If he has gone, ja.'

'Beifeld,' I said, turning back from going to leave, 'Isn't that the name of a place round here?'

'It was a schloss many years ago, but blown up in the war with the RAF. It is now but a name. Nothing there but ruins.'

So I went. The Steins had not agreed on Munt at all, but this could be because Munt liked the woman, and couldn't stand the man.

Beifeld was of great importance now. It was more than a telephone exchange. It had been a place in the forest worth the RAF's time and energy to blow it up.

What had it been, then?

When I got out into the street, a police car was waiting outside the police office. I went into the office and there was a patrolman and a constable of some rank I couldn't fathom. I told them who I was and they looked at me as if judging what sort of criminal I might be.

Then one laughed and they went on smoking cigars and talked about a few things, the sort of things they usually ask tourists.

Then I asked what The Schloss at Beifeld had been.

They looked at each other. They must have been very young when the castle was blown.

'It was I think, the headquarters of some organisation, secret service, you call it? I think it was for that.'

'Or perhaps to do with rockets?' the patrolman said. 'I do not know for sure. It was military. That is certain. You wish to go there?'

'I would like to have a look. I'm interested in architecture, even just the ruins.'

So he told me how to get there.

And it was a different way from that the garagier had told me.

Life is full of surprises, I thought as I went out.

I ought to have mentioned Haynes, but there was hardly enough of him left to bother about.

By then I had quite decided not to bother with the police, to put it quietly. The things Marthe Stein had said made me feel that my instinct had been right; that Munt was not a baddie.

I got into the car and went back to the garage. The cheese came bouncing forth once more, beaming.

'I forgot,' I said, 'my phone went off. Would you report it? I don't know who to do it to.'

'Of course, of course,' he said. 'You are happy, otherwise?'

'Quite happy,' I said. 'Just tell me again the way to Beifeld.'

So he told me again. It was the same as he had said before and different from the police version.

'Is that where there was once a castle?' I said.

'That is not far,' he said. 'Yes.'

I got the map out and made him point out the track.

'It is not good road, you understand,' he said. 'It is in a state of neglect. I think it was once part of the Schloss estate grounds.'

As he pointed it I saw another dotted double track which coincided with the way the police had said. Where the two ways joined there was a Chelsea bun of dotted lines indicating the ruins of the castle.

I left him and chose his way. I did that because I was suspicious of it for some reason; I suppose the main being that the police, giving a certain way, could have no axe to grind.

The garagier, on the other hand, hadn't even mentioned the castle, just the brick telephone box.

The way was a track, not bad, but through the sandy soil of the pine country nothing much seems to happen by way of overgrowing.

By the map it read about six kilometres, but somehow it felt much longer. The forest was quiet, undisturbed and even in the bright morning, somehow dark. Here and there straggly rhododendron bushes reached hopelessly upwards to try and penetrate the roof formed by the firs.

There was no definite mark I could see to show the track was ever used, but here and there faded food cartons lay around, proving tourists came now and then.

I came to a clearing, where there was some rough grass and a hard standing in front of a small concrete building bearing the telefun title.

Leading to it from the direction the police had pointed out to me was a hard road of broken stone.

I stopped and got out, looking round me.

Then I saw a man hurrying towards me, a big man, like a hippopotamus with a black sweep's brush on his head.

SIX

1

The man came into the clearing smoking a thick cigar. The blue floated after him in small clouds as he puffed along. He wore a long white overall, which was dirty and stained with paint of various colours.

He glowered at me, or in my direction, and then grinned as if it were merely an exercise to aerate his forty-eight front teeth.

He lumbered towards me, covering the ground surprisingly quickly, considering his ungainliness.

Then without any further sign of recognition that anyone was there, he swept by, leaving me with a cloud of blue smoke in my face.

He shambled on and into the trees by the side of a break in them where the track went on through.

In a life of surprises I think that non-reaction to me being there was one of the sharpest. He just ambled in amongst the trees and the sounds of his shoes and noisy puffing died away. I was left with the birds.

I was also left with a degree of nonplus. I

had met the hippopotamus man and he had ignored me in an open space, just walked by – almost through me.

Yet I had instinctive feelings that he had known who I was. I had no reason for that, except that if he hadn't known, I think he would have stopped to ask.

I waited a while but my lonely peace was uninterrupted. The track went round a bend and over the brow of a hill. I walked down it until I could see over the brow.

The track wound down between the trees and finally became lost under them. And, like a big sore in the carpet of trees below me, there was an open space, round in shape, with the ragged broken teeth of stone ruins sticking up from the ground. There were a few walls still standing, just sheets of wall with empty windows, like the flat front of a film set.

It had been well clobbered in that old air attack. It must have been important to have earned a plastering like this.

The ruins were some way down there, so I went back and drove down to the fringe of the clearing. It was a dried up moat, now overgrown with bushes and thicket. The stone bridge going across to the broken walls still stood but with large lumps of it blown away. Weeds grew up in the cracks.

I walked across and into the grass grown ruins. It was eerie. A lot of furniture, broken and lurching, still lay around amidst the fallen stone, entwined now with climbing weeds.

A flock of crows flew up from some empty upper openings in a standing wall and cawed raucously, as if they didn't like me.

Beifeld. This was Beifeld. What was the 12?

Twelve is in some legends a magic number. I didn't think it would apply here, though this was a country thick with legends.

There were also secret service numbers, but this was hardly likely to be one as it had been bandied about by a loose tongued American pressure man.

It was hot in that place, and after the crows had gone over to some trees, quiet. As I wandered slowly through the ruins there was now and again the rustle of some little animals wriggling off through the weeds.

I came into a ruined passage, where the sun streamed down through the broken arched roof and the edges of the wrecked stone above me were etched on the paving stones in deep shadow.

And as I watched the ugly serrated line of the breaks one part moved.

I looked up. The edges of the stone, some with weeds hanging down in trailers, were all undisturbed. Yet a yard or two back from where I stood a pair of the trailing weeds were spinning slowly in the still air.

Naturally no one showed up there, and I wiped my face and walked slowly on, looking around me tripper-wise.

Now and again I saw a slight movement on the serrated edge of the shadow. Somebody was up there following.

The thought did strike me that it might be a large bird or animal of some sort, say a rat, but I had the feeling that it wasn't.

I remembered the spiderman as I moved out of the end of the broken cloister into a wider space of broken stone lying in a sea of weed and rough grass.

Looking back then I could see something of the wrecked wall above the passage. Nothing moved there until suddenly I heard a pop or crack from behind me.

Instantly something moved on the broken roof and a man shambled away at very high speed, considering the surface he was on.

Only a spiderman could have done such a journey so fast.

I turned. A dark haired girl was clambering over fallen stones towards me.

'Hi! Johnny! Wait for me!'

She came up, rather breathless and laughing as she dropped an air pistol into the satchel bag slung from her shoulder.

'Remember me?' she said brightly.

'I never forget beautiful girls who consistently try to get me shot,' I said.

'Oh, that time in Spain,' she said lightly.

'Well, I was young then, you know. Eighteen, but.'

'And now you're nineteen and responsible?' I said.

'Oh, much,' she said.

I looked back to the broken roof, but the spiderman had gone.

'Why did you shoot the man?' I said.

'It wasn't a man, it was a monkey,' she said. 'He looked as if he was going to sling a stone at your head.'

'In which case, thanks.' I watched her. 'And what are you doing here?'

'Following you,' she said, as if surprised I didn't know.

'What?'

'You need protection,' she said. 'You don't really know where you're at, do you?'

'I don't see how you know.'

'Nobody ever sees how I know anything,' she said and laughed. 'You know this is a dangerous place, don't you? Why do you always choose hot spots for your picnics, darling?'

I sat on a stone and offered a cigarette which she took. We had met in Spain and got highly involved with an unhappy band of international crooks, and as a result of her behaviour I've never been able to make up my mind about what she really is. Agent, fool, flirt, mischievous imp? All those, now I came to think of it.

'You take things too lightly,' she said, looking down at me, her head cocked. 'You surely don't really think Munt and Lilli went off by themselves, do you?'

That shook me.

'How do you know about them?' I said.

'I found out. That's my job.'

'You've actually got a job?'

'I had one before.'

She looked around. The birds had got used to us for they were singing all round and, circling above the highest point of the brown walls, the crows cawed.

'What do you think happened to those two?' I said.

'They were collared. The abominable snowmen. You saw them last night.'

'You intrigue me,' I said. 'How do you know I saw them?'

'I'm a mind reader. But they've got your friends, or tenants or whatever they are.'

Up to that time I had thought the pair had found it better all round to get out before a lot of small legal offences came to light regarding tenancies and misappropriation of rent.

If they had been snatched during the night, that was a different matter.

For I had been in the house as well, and left quite alone. This was heartening, for it meant that up to this morning nobody wanted to do me in. By sticking my nose in further, as I had done since, I might have changed their almost benevolent attitude towards me.

The other benevolent attitude – Kate's, as I remembered her name – was harder to explain.

'Tell me what you know,' I said.

'A man said to me, "Johnny Blake has gone to Bavaria to see a property which came with the old man's estate, and this property is hot", the man said.'

She smiled and sat down beside me.

'What man?'

'A man in London who finds out things.'

I could see there wasn't much point in pushing that one, at least, for a while. I remembered that it was almost impossible to get anything out of Kate. She had a mental agility like a wriggling fish.

'What do you mean – hot?' I said.

'Munt has been working there for some years, and there was a leakthrough he'd made a breakthrough, and this put him on the hot spot. There were a lot of people waiting to see if he could do it, and if he did, they were ready to go in and get it.'

'Is that what you're after?'

'No. I'm after you.' She laughed.

'How did you follow me here?'

'You're not too hard to follow, are you? You go all through the village asking questions about where you're going next.'

Too easy.

'Did you see a man like a hippopotamus in the forest?'

'No, but that's the man you must keep clear of.'

'Was Bauer one of his names?'

'I think it was. Yes, I'm sure it was. I haven't got the list but I think that was one.'

'What's the meaning of Beifeld 12?'

She cocked her head.

'New to me. Is it a phone number?'

I told her what I thought it wasn't.

'And this man Haynes gave it away?'

'He boasted about the power it lent his elbow.'

'If that power was whipped away under his feet, it sounds like the man you call Bauer. He does that for laughs.'

'He sounds a generous character,' I said and told her about the hand.

'Ugh! Yes. That's Bauer's giggle all right.'

'You speak with me?'

He had come very silently for one so large and clumsy. We did not look round at once, but when we did, there was the hippo man, sucking at a fat cigar.

2

'We did mention you, yes,' I said.

This was asking for it, but I felt he knew

108

about us anyway, so it didn't make much difference. Kate laughed in a soft, very amused manner.

'What is it we talk of?'

'Beifeld,' I said.

'Ah.' Bauer waved his cigar about and shrugged. 'Das ist hier.'

'Was,' I said.

'Big battering. Smashing time,' said Bauer and suddenly roared with laughter. He pointed up to the remaining walls. 'I show you bones still stuck up there where they were blown into the stones. Very interesting for diggers many centuries hence.'

'Do you like this place?' Kate said.

'We all like it, yes?' Bauer said, looking for our agreement.

'Do you come here often?' she said.

'I come when my friends come,' he said. 'So now I am here.' He smiled with ferocious geniality. 'I think we all look for the same thing. Eh? Happiness perhaps. The eternal search. Is that what we seek?'

'As a matter of fact,' I said, 'I'm looking for my late tenant, Doctor Frankenstein. There are certain matters he forgot.'

'That is most satisfactory,' Bauer said, nodding. 'I, too, look for him. But his name, as you know, is Munt. He had to change names to get on with his work uninterrupted. He was followed by a desperate organisation. But he did not know they would leave him until he had succeeded with his work.'

'They left him alone until he did succeed?'

'Naturally. They are not doctors. They cannot carry on where he might leave off. So they wait, you see. Munt gets used to this waiting. Finally he believes that there is nobody after him at all.'

'When did he find out?' I said.

'When I told him,' Bauer said, taking a deep draught of smoke. 'I called on him and warned him. He got mad and there was a fight.' He chuckled.

'Why ever did he get mad?' said Kate with lovely innocence.

'He thinks I am telling a lot of lies. When a man is on the threshold of success his nerves are very much stretched. One makes allowances.'

'How did you know enough to warn him?' Kate said.

'I was once in the same position,' Bauer said. 'I know what it is like. But to defend myself then I had to find out who was trying to get at me. I did find out but I did not let anybody know. You understand me? So that the operators themselves did not know I was thereafter able to watch them. It has been a defensive pastime for me, and of no other use until I discovered that Munt was on the point of being pumped, as you say.'

Anything more open, frank and genially confidential I had not come across. I began to doubt what I had heard of Bauer and to think that obviously, there was more than one Bauer.

It was quite impossible to tell from Kate's flirtatious interest just what she thought of the hippo man.

'And what brought you here?' she asked. 'Have you some gen that these operators are here somewhere?' She looked round. 'It doesn't look a very promising headquarters, I must say.'

'I understand it is more useful than it looks,' he said, mouthing a lot of rich smoke before blowing it out in a long, thick lipped trail.

'You mean the bombers didn't hit the heart?' I said.

'The Nazis had much of an obsession with bunkers, you may remember,' he said. 'There is supposed to be a certain security underground. It is the fear wish to return to the safety of the womb, for God knows, bunkers are as unsafe as anywhere else.'

His eyes moved in their pouchy bags, sliding from side to side, as if searching the ruins for a sign of a hidden entrance.

'Suppose that we look around,' he said, making a circle in the air with his cigar. 'It can do no harm. It may help.'

So we started clambering and probing the ruins and the weeds and getting nowhere. Very often I looked around and up to the highest parts of the broken walls but saw no more of the spiderman.

'There's a somewhat peculiar creature,' I said when we stopped for a rest. 'He climbs straight up walls and has got the reputation of being a wolf man.'

'Legend. Yokel talk,' said Bauer contemptuously.

'But I've seen him,' I said. 'I've even chased him.'

Bauer's eyes squeezed almost shut. He reminded me of the cheeselike garagier.

'That is interesting,' he said. 'I thought the fools had made him up.'

It seemed he didn't know about the spiderman or this was another act in his so far impeccable performance as the honest fighter for freedom against thuggery.

'Didn't Munt mention him?' I said.

'Munt did not want to talk to me,' Bauer said and grinned. 'He was what you might call reluctant, rude, violently opposed. He thought I was a rival after his brains.'

This was close to what Munt had said himself about people stealing his brains. Anyone, else, I thought, would have said work, invention, discovery, but Munt had said brains.

As if the real secret of his discovery was still inside his head.

In which case, he had been kidnapped in order to have the information taken out of his head. Which seemed to make the matter urgent.

'You know this organisation,' I said. 'Who are they?'

'One doesn't know the identities,' Bauer said, smoking slowly. 'Just that it is an operative company which seeks new discoveries and offers them for sale.'

'You must have seen some of these operatives?' I said.

'I have seen them, yes. But they wear such uniforms.' He shrugged.

'The snowmen?'

'It is a useful dress, considering what they do.'

'Raise fires?' I said.

'Usually, that is the last act. They search everything, take what may help and burn the rest. It destroys all. The evidence of what the discovery was, and the identity of those stealing it.'

He grinned.

'And where is the meeting place or are there several?'

'I think one is here. I think there is a bunker, but I do not know.'

By this time we had gone all round the plan of the ruins and looked down the slopes outside into the overgrown moat. From above one can usually see if the undergrowth has been recently broken through, but there was no sign that we had seen.

'What gave you the idea it was here?' I said.

'The Beifeld, of course,' he said. 'It was once a centre of intrigue, so why not again?'

'If I had a centre of intrigue and knew it might be bombed so I had to build a bunker I wouldn't build the bunker near the place but somewhere else and a way to get to the centre if necessary,' Kate said gaily.

'That is most sensible,' said Bauer. 'But were they so sensible? We look afterwards at the event of the bombing, but before it is not so easy to be sensible.'

And then I remembered the hiding-place under my own floor where intriguers had hidden long before any bombing was contemplated.

It had produced a different kind of bunker; not a protection place but a hiding-place.

I did not trust Bauer, despite his genial frankness. I kept remembering what had been said about him, and that this man, though he seemed different, could be the same doing a fine act.

The possibility was that he was deliberately misleading us. He might know where the bunker was and lead us right away from it in a fruitless search to waste our time and energy and persuade us that nothing was there.

Which is one of the drawbacks of meeting a dog with a bad name. You start thinking about him before you have anything real to go on, so that you begin to be uncertain about everything that comes up afterwards.

Was he good or was he bad? If I could make up my mind about that we might know where we stood.

I was worried about Munt. Despite his deadpan attitude he must have had something, some shine of sincerity or despair that had persuaded me.

Or perhaps it was that, having believed he had sloped off on his own, taking Lilli for company, his situation had suddenly switched to be the persecuted party. I always tend to slide for the persecuted party. That's why I get into so much trouble.

With my companions, whom I didn't want, I felt confined. I even felt they had deliberately piled on my back to stop me finding out for myself.

Each would have a different reason, I realised, but their effect would be the same.

But to escape from two apparent friends seemed twice as hard as from enemies.

'Now,' said Kate, very chummily to Bauer, 'suppose we find this bunker, what do we do?'

'It is of value to know the fox's run,' said the hippoman. 'After that, one chooses the time.'

'But isn't there some urgency?' she said, somewhat surprised. 'I mean, Munt is a valuable man for peace in the world, isn't he?'

'Indeed, indeed,' he said, nodding his big shaggy head.

'Suppose,' she said, 'that the warmongers get him. Couldn't they turn what he has done to benefit the aims of the force merchants?'

'Indeed, this could be done, so far as I understand what he was working at,' said Bauer, thoughtfully. 'But remember, I do not know it all.'

'You must have an idea,' she said.

'That is very easy,' Bauer said. 'It is the harnessing of natural forces to negative the effects of combat weapons. To nullify the effect of arms.'

'What about hands?' I said sharply.

He cocked his head and squeezed his eyes at me.

'Bitte?' he said.

'Miss it,' I said.

'Then these operators,' said Kate quickly, 'would be buyers and sellers. Not nationals spying on each other.'

Bauer laughed sardonically.

'My dear, there is very little money in spying for one's own country these days. They even quibble over the widow's pension.'

I looked up over the broken roof of the cloisters, I thought I caught a movement up there, but when I stared, saw nothing animated but the birds wheeling high up over the wreck of a high wall.

If the spiderman was around, he could hear everything we said for the day was quiet and the interior of the ruins rather like an amphitheatre for sound.

'What do you look for?' Bauer said sharply.

'I thought someone moved up there,' I said.

The hippo man stared a moment, then began to clamber slowly back over the stones, puffing quickly but regularly on his cigar.

'Is he ours or not?' I whispered. 'Hippo, I mean?'

She shook her head.

We watched Bauer come to a halt about ten yards from where the cloisters began. He took the cigar from his mouth and tilted his head to look up. It looked like a tufted ball rolling on a sandbag.

He stayed like that, without moving. We watched the smoke spiralling lazily from the cigar in his hand.

'He seems to be struck like it,' Kate breathed in my ear. 'Is he going into a trance?'

I didn't answer. I was fascinated by the absolute stillness of the listening, watching machine by the cloisters. There was something terrifying about the cold, inhuman patience of the watcher. Whatever else he was, this cruel and motionless wait was somehow evil.

The bottom corner of his dirty white coat moved a little in a light wind as if restless with the wait and the cigar smoke suddenly whizzed away past his arm.

We also watched that broken line of stone against the sky, but I saw nothing and from her tenseness of expectation I guessed she didn't, either.

A bird started up from a hole in a stone wall with a sudden buzz and chatter of falling stone dust. It made her jump. I looked round to make sure what it had been.

Bauer, monstrous cat at the hole, did not move at all.

I began to feel sick. My feelings turned against him and started in pity for whatever he was after.

Kate bent suddenly and picked up a stone big as a golf ball. She held it in her fists and stood tensed, watching either the broken roof or Bauer. I couldn't tell.

And then it came, a very slow cautious movement, a rim of different colour beyond the broken edge of stone.

Still Bauer did not move. Kate drew back her hand. The shadow became a head, turning to dart back along the dangerous roof.

I have never seen anything so quick as

Bauer then. His empty right hand snatched a pistol from his pocket, took aim and fired, all it seemed in the same movement.

It would have blown the shadow's head off, but for one thing.

As Bauer snatched the gun, Kate threw her stone at Bauer.

And she hit him right under the ear.

SEVEN

1

Bauer staggered. I saw the shadow on the broken roof scuttling away, little bits of stone and sprays of dust falling over the edge as he went.

'Oh, I'm terribly sorry!' Kate cried out. 'I'm afraid I'm not a very good shot. I didn't mean to hit you.'

Bauer just stood with the gun hanging to his side and his head bent, his left hand trying to cover it. His fallen cigar burned lazily where he had stood before the shot.

I watched the roof but saw no more than the little tumbles of stone and dust.

The question which fascinated me then was why Bauer had shot like that. He had meant to kill. The last second snatch, the flick aim, dead sure, crack-shot type had been meant to hit home.

Even with that kind of shot, at the distance of a few feet a good shot couldn't have missed.

But why kill the spy up there? Spies are handier alive if you want to know something.

The only answer to this riddle could be

that Bauer already knew everything the spy knew and didn't want us to know.

So that put him where I had believed him to be before he had put on the bareface act of innocence.

He dropped his hand and looked round. I think the cover had been less to comfort his pain in the ear than to hide the fury which he felt, but which would not go with his act.

'So sorry,' said Kate again.

Bauer shrugged and slipped the gun back into the pocket of his dirty white overall.

'It cannot be helped,' he said.

I watched either end of the broken gallery but did not see anyone climb down from above. There must be a way up that was not visible outwardly.

Bauer turned away from the cloisters. Kate watched him. I looked on past them, still wondering where the escaper had gone.

And then I saw him. The picture was through a crack in the masonry which gave a small snapshot of the outer rim of the dried-up moat.

The man appeared, scuttling up the brambly slope, more like a spider than ever. He wound in amongst wild bushes and then, quite suddenly disappeared into the bank.

No trace was left. No track showed that such a way had been used before. It was a piece of neat, natural camouflage.

I noted the crack in the wall was in line with a tree on the edge of the track where my car stood.

'He's just disappeared,' Kate said. 'Was he spying?'

Bauer was about to speak but I cut in.

'The poor fellow's a lunatic,' I said. 'He scrabbles about like a spider, climbs things, hides from people. I don't see him being used as a spy by any responsible group.'

Bauer stared at me a moment, and then shrugged.

'Perhaps you are right,' he said. 'Who can tell?'

My problem of how to get rid of the pair of companions was now urgent. I wanted badly to find that entrance in the moat bank, but no longer had any wish to let Bauer see me do it.

The shot had aligned Bauer where I had first thought him. As far as Kate was concerned, I have never been able to decide which side she is on, if she ever is quite sure herself.

Possibly she did work for someone, but whatever work she did was always swung unexpectedly by her whims and sudden desire to have something for herself. This made it very difficult to apply rules of judgment to her.

Whether Bauer was dazed or not I didn't know, but he walked away for a short distance, shaking his head slowly.

Kate came close to me when I wagged a finger at her.

'Occupy the fat one while I get around,' I said. 'Keep him here.'

'Did you see him get away?'

'I think so. I want to know for sure.'

'Trust me, darling. Make it quick.'

I ducked in behind a bit of wall and went round through the weeds towards the slope down to the moat.

I heard Bauer say, 'Where did he go?'

Kate said, 'To his car for something.'

They began to talk together about the man on the roof, she making weird suggestions as to what had happened to him.

Once in the overgrown bottom of the moat I pushed on round to the other side of Beifeld, where I had seen the spiderman vanish.

Looking up I got the rent in the wall but couldn't see the tree over the lip of the moat wall, so I climbed the slope a bit on the castle side until I got the tree in line.

The weeds and bushes on the opposite side of the moat showed no sign of where the man had gone in. The camouflage was extraordinarily good.

I crossed the bottom of the trench and began to climb the outer side, looking back, now and again, up to the ruins to see if Kate had failed to hold Bauer.

It seemed she hadn't, but the seem was wrong, as it turned out. Bauer wasn't as simple as to watch what I was doing and let me see him.

Going up that slope the secret of the entrance became obvious. The way ahead showed like a small tunnel formed by the overgrowing bushes, so that anyone going upwards from there could not be seen because of the roof of greenery over him.

I went up, crawling on the face of the moat wall to where there was a square entrance, formed with concrete, but thick and bumpy now with the earth of many years.

The concrete lining went in four or five feet, a sort of blast trap, and at the end was an iron door. This had a spinwheel on it, like the door of a safe or the bulkhead control in a submarine.

It turned easily and made no noise. It pushed in heavily but smoothly. The whole thing was kept oiled for instant use.

Inside it was dark. No surprise. The surprise was that the air smelt quite fresh, a thing not usually found in bunkers unless they have air conditioners in operation.

I listened and in the darkness I could hear the faint hum of machines pumping air somewhere.

The direction of the run of the black tunnel headed back underneath the telephone exchange, if it ran almost straight.

I went in on hands and knees for the entrance was only about that square. As the greenish light through the overgrowth faded behind me, the darkness did not increase.

A similar light seemed to be fading in from somewhere ahead of me. It was so diffused that for some seconds I did not believe it was a light, but some sort of phosphorescence ahead.

When it grew a little stronger I thought the tunnel must come out into the open again through a similar mass of growth at the entrance.

I could see enough to stand upright and felt the roughness of a concrete wall either side of me.

My progress was not quick. I kept stopping to listen in case the spiderman was somewhere ahead and waiting for me. But I heard nothing beyond the faint humming of the air fans.

I didn't fancy the idea of meeting him in the gloom. There is always something rather frightening about the unusual and the malformed. A relic of childhood fears, but inclined to be real in the dark.

The light became, not so much stronger as plainer, as if some underground sun was about to rise. Then I heard voices.

They were weird, echoing in the concrete warren, so that a single word repeated on itself like a blurred photograph.

Worse still for me, it was in German.

I remember being irritated about that detail, though I might well have expected it.

If it hadn't echoed so badly I might have got the gist, if it hadn't echoed so badly I might have been able to recognise at least the voices. As it was it was like the sound track of an outer space film.

There was an opening just ahead and on the right of the passage. I peered round the corner and down a flight or concrete steps. They seemed to lead into a room, but the lintel cut off all view of it except a small area of floor round the foot of the stairs.

The light was much stronger down there, and the voices were chattering from beyond the area I could see.

If I went down to see who, they would also see who, so I stayed at the top.

And then from the echoing chatter I began to make out one word because it was repeated several times and then was followed by silence.

The word seemed to be 'Einzwei' and even my knowledge of the language told me it was 'one-two'. I got a spasm of excitement thinking I was at last tapping the one-two of Beifeld.

But nobody answered the silences that followed the einzwei, and then, after a few calls like this, the conversation was resumed.

Further, another conversation joined it, but

didn't seem to communicate with the first one. Like four people talking across each other. Then I began to hear other voices, seeming further off down the room.

The talks started, stopped, and then others came on.

Then I began to suspect that down there somebody was tapping the lines of the telephone exchange in the forest of Beifeld.

I took a good look through the gloom down the corridor on each side of me and then doubled-up pretty well, and crept down the stairs.

Further in the room there were festoons of cables in bunches looping down from the ceiling and what looked like computers with slow rolling tapes in glass cases.

I couldn't see anyone in attendance.

It looked like an automatic recording system for the conversations going through the exchange. But what talk from a country area could be worth such an expensive layout as this?

You could operate a by-product, I supposed, like selling certain tapes to blackmailers but the income from that couldn't be enough.

The voices went on chattering and cutting off as I tried to guess what was behind this elaborate tapping and taping system.

It was a wrong place to guess.

I got the instinct or the smell of someone

behind me. I turned and looked up the stairs as the great bag of hair and wild white teeth came down at me.

I twisted and he went past my chest and hit the wall sliding crash as he went on down to the floor of the tape room.

But twisting on a stair is a fool's game. My feet jammed against the riser and trying to free them I stumbled and started to reel down the rest of the flight.

The spiderman came up on his feet like something pushing up from the ground. I got to the bottom of the flight and backed to the wall on one side.

But he didn't come for me this time. Instead he went down on all fours and scampered away behind the machines.

I didn't like the manoeuvre in that grim, dim light, which was coming, in fact from the glass cases of the machines themselves.

The chattering of voices continued as I went cautiously forward along the side wall, trying to see where he was hiding, but the odd lights made it too confusing to be sure of something as just a shadow and not someone hiding. The machines were not set out in any geometrical form but just stood around anyhow in no sort of pattern, which made it worse.

And then from one of the chattering machines I heard a voice which held me fixed where I stood. Not because I knew it but because of what it said.

'Jonathan Blake,' it chittered, 'get out of that place while you can.'

All in perfectly plain English. The rest of the chattering went on and the warning voice went back to nothing.

2

My wish to obey the voice was strong, but I couldn't start to go with a man hiding behind my back. It was essential to clear him up first.

A game of hide and seek in that light, with an opponent who didn't even move like an ordinary man was a chilly idea. It chilled me as I backed along the wall, trying to get the view behind each scattered machine.

The voices, chittering away all the time, with accompanying clicks and pauses helped to confuse the senses by a kind of three dimensional sound effect coming even from the blank wall behind me.

The rolling tape spools in the cabinet gleamed in their own light, flickering as they turned so that the dim light they shed outside was alive with movement.

I kept thinking I saw him crouching in the moving shadows among the machines, but another flicker from a spool could show up nothing there.

The sweat began to break out. The confusing web of noise was getting into my head and trying to make me dizzy.

I came to the corner of the wall at the far end from the stairs and looked behind the uneven bank of machines. Once again I thought I saw him. I was getting impatient then, bursting to have a go even if it turned out to be a shadow in the end.

I went towards the cabinet, but as I got to the nearest one I had a horrid sensation of someone being behind me and I glanced round.

I was wrong. No one was behind me but someone was on the stairs swinging something in his hand. I recognised Munt from the way he stood there, and the curious stiff-necked attitude he had.

In the second my glance took me the spiderman grabbed me from behind and low down. He got me fair and square and I went down with him on top of me, heavy as a gorilla.

Just about then the whole room lit up with a searing burst of flame and the crack of the explosion was like thunder in the ears. The air filled with electric flashes, the screaming of machines running amok inside themselves and the racketing echoes of the explosion.

As the sharper thunder faded off there were numerous crashes as machines toppled and fell against each other. The chittering voices were stilled at last.

The stench of smoke, explosive and burning rubber came chokingly from every quarter.

The explosion had stunned me, and perhaps spiderman, too for he just laid on top of me for several seconds and then got off quickly.

I sat up amongst the smoking debris.

He barked at me in German and pointed towards the back of the room, the nearest wall to where we were. Fire was spreading amongst the machines and the smoke and smell made it hard to breathe, or even to keep the eyes clear of tears. I had to blink to see him make the gesture towards the back wall.

I clambered over red hot metal and could even feel the heat through the soles of my shoes. I fell against the wall.

He went through an opening a few feet away from me, and with a few more blinks and holding my breath to stop the foul air choking me, I got there and through.

Once on the other side it was cooler and the stench was thinner. A door slammed behind me and I put my back against the passage wall in case he tried to get at my weakest point.

In the shock and confusion of the big bang I hadn't quite got round to the idea that he might not have been meaning to attack me, but had saved me from a bomb he knew was on its way.

It was pitch dark, but gradually my eyes cleared enough to see a little square of light away to my left. It looked like daylight.

Thinning clouds of black smoke were drifting towards it. Ducking below the smoke, and using his fantastic animal movement, the spiderman was hurrying towards that exit.

That shook me, too. Having covered me from the blast he seemed to have lost interest in everything but getting out of it fast.

I followed him. He had been helpful once and might be again.

He went out of the opening and vanished. The light was green, shining through vegetation as at the entrance. I had no doubt this place was well camouflaged from all angles.

Then as I went towards that freedom I saw a man, or rather the lower part of a man. Spiderman had gone to the right. This man came from the left. He made a slow step forward and stopped filling the opening. He stood quite still holding a Luger in his right hand. He held it as if he meant to use it.

I stopped. There was an opening in the wall a yard ahead of me on the left. I went on, very quietly, and slipped into it. It had a door which was open.

There was a peculiar smell from the

darkness behind me, but I was intent upon watching the gunman and it didn't register then.

He bent and looked in at the tunnel. I saw him sniff. He had caught the stink of the explosion drifting up the passage.

He looked the way spiderman had gone, and then came into the passage and once inside, straightened and hurried along down to the tapping room.

I watched him go into the gloom and reach the door. He opened it. A whole blasting cloud of flame and smoke rolled out as if to swallow him.

In its murky glare I saw him struggle with the door and finally get it shut. Then he ran hard back to the exit, ducked and fled out.

He was not running from the fire. He was running to tell somebody what had happened.

So that soon more than one man would come back. The disaster might bring all the people concerned in this extensive tapping operation.

It depended on how far he had to go as to whether I would have time to get away or not. If running now meant I would walk into the arms of an angry organisation who thought I'd blown their pet spy station then it was best not to run but to wait a bit.

The rotten smell behind me became noticeable even with the acrid stink in front of me in the passage.

I thought I recognised it and it made me decide to get out whatever the time handicap might be. I ran to the exit, held a moment, peering out through the leaves and then pushed out into the forest.

Through the trees I could see the squat telephone building because the gathering of a large number of pine trees don't hide very much.

They could only hide me if I ran from one to another and I could easily be seen in between. I looked round to where the concrete exit was hidden in the bank. There was a lot of aged, stringy foliage around that bank, no doubt specially planted many years ago and grown scraggy and tough with time.

They were nearly all stalk now and didn't hide much. The exit cover was probably planted there for the purpose much more recently.

At the first quick glance round it seemed the only place to hide was the telephone exchange, which was locked.

Then some way off, but sounding clear amongst the trees I heard men shouting. I guessed what they were shouting about and made off the opposite way, away from the exchange and back towards the ruins.

That way lay up the bank and I scrambled up through the tough old vegetation until my trouser legs were torn to shreds and not a little bloody.

But from on top there was cover by the very angle at the edge of the fall and I stopped there and looked back through the trees.

I saw three men running towards the hidden exit. Further behind a VW was bumping in and out amongst the trees, following the men on foot.

Not one of the men was Bauer.

I think I felt disappointed about that, except that if one had been the jovial butcher, then I would have Kate to worry about.

Not one of the men had a gun in his hand and no other obvious weapon was visible.

I backed down from the bank, watching through the twiggy cover. The men ran like mad for the covered exit and reached it in a pack which pulled them to a halt.

They shouted one to another, probably about the fumes of fire from inside. One man called back to the VW which had then stopped. The driver had got out and stood at the open door, watching the group.

The call seemed to be for fire extinguishers, for the driver ducked his head and shoulders into the car and came out with three small ones. He ran these to the others and three went in, leaving the driver to stand sentry at the exit.

I looked back through the trees to the ruins standing in the sun. I had the idea someone was there and kept low in the straggly growth.

Nothing happened for a minute or more, then I saw someone clambering up the side of the moat a long way back. The head came into view and it made me move quickly away from the sentinel below me.

Once clear of the undergrowth I ran across the soft pine carpet towards the girl as she swung along towards me. When she saw me running, she stopped and waited.

'What have you done?' she said as I stopped by her.

'The damn place has blown up in there,' I said. 'And I've a feeling they think I did it.'

'Well, didn't you?' She cocked her head and looked quizzical.

'No. I saw a man throw a grenade down there and I think it was Munt.'

'Munt?' She looked startled. 'Then he's not been taken prisoner?'

'Seems not. Seems also that he knew Beifeld 12 after all.'

'Then where's Lilli?'

'I don't know where either of them are. I just saw Munt alone on the steps.'

'He didn't mean to do you, did he?' she said. 'I mean you're sure he did it just to wreck the headquarters?'

'I hadn't thought of it,' I said. 'It naturally seemed sensible for a man like Munt to destroy the spy system. After all, they were after his discovery. I'm not after anything.'

'You have the unfortunate ability to look as though you are,' she said.

I looked back through the trees but there was no sign of activity. Probably the men below were fighting the fire in the hope of saving something.

'What did you do with Bauer?' I said.

'Oh that,' she said, and looked the other way.

'What did you do with him?' I persisted.

'Clunked him,' she said, lightly. 'What else was there to do in the circumstances?'

'What circumstances?'

'He tried to make me tell where you'd gone,' she said. 'Now, I don't like being forced to do anything. It's against my easy-going nature.'

'Just paint the picture.'

'He started asking me. Then he got my arm and twisted it, so I let him, you know, till he thought he was really giving me the screw. Then I turned on it, you know and put my knee in his fat tummy. So he let go.'

'Then what?'

'He sort of staggered sideways and I saw he was staggering and keeping his right side away from me and I remembered the right pocket was where he had put the gun. And presto! Out it came – or nearly.'

'Because why?'

'Because when I got suspicious of the way

137

he reeled like that I picked up a piece of old gargoyle that weighed about thirty good pounds and tapped his head with it. I think he shot himself or something.'

'Oh blimey!' I said. 'You haven't left corpses lying about? Remember this is Germany. We'll be pinched and held and questioned and goodness knows–'

'Don't panic. He's not dead,' she said sweetly. 'Just out on a psychedelic trip. He'll be back.'

She pointed suddenly.

'In fact,' she said, 'he's back now.'

And then we heard Bauer's bull voice bellowing with rage and calling for somebody.

EIGHT

1

We watched Bauer storming the battlements, as you might say, by standing there and bellowing from amid the ruins. His voice echoed in the forest like a trumpeting elephant's, but for a while nothing seemed to happen.

Kate turned to me suddenly then, as if she had found something useful in the scene.

'Is the exchange down there totally destroyed?' she said.

'I should say completely. It was a handy bomb Munt threw in.'

'You know what?' she said looking back to Bauer.

'What?'

'We must get back to Karen. Now!'

'It isn't going to be easy. We wouldn't stand a chance on foot and the car's on the wrong side of the sympathisers, who won't take long to see what the damage is down there.'

'It's got to be the car – before Bauer gets off the castle.'

'So be ready for a sharp sprint,' I said.

'The cover's only trees. They won't hide us but they will jazz up a gunshot so that he couldn't hit.'

'I'd forgotten you were an expert. Let's go.'

From her attitude I knew she knew something, and her hunches and bits of information, I had learnt, weren't to be disregarded. She had been snooping around near Karen, as I had, and from what she decided then about going back, I guessed she had found out more than I had.

So we ran, dodging from tree to tree and keeping apart, running at different times and speeds so that one confused the movements of the other. I got her to cooperate by calling out when to go, when to ease, when to stop behind a tree.

It was as well we did it this way because Bauer caught sight of us from where he stood at a break in the castle wall. I saw that gun glint in his hand as he pointed it towards us. But he didn't fire. He was too mean to waste a shot firing in amongst the trees.

Yet he would be ready when we broke cover by the car, and he must have been able to see we were heading for it.

When we got within fifty yards of the vehicle, we heard shouts from behind us echoing up into the trees.

The salvage squad were out again, angry at what they had found.

As we ran I noticed one favourable point for us. The track on which the car stood was higher than the ground on which Bauer was. He was looking up at the Mercedes. The top was down.

Kate and I stopped together just before the last lap.

'Run zigzag for the far side of the car,' I said.

So she started off and so did I. She zigged and zagged while I ran on the side of her Bauer was on, covering as far as possible.

It was a twenty yard sprint, no more.

A couple of shots came from the castle and hit somewhere up in the trees. We got to the cover of the car side as some answering shots came down from the salvage gang.

So everybody was armed, though I had not seen any sign of guns when they had arrived.

We crouched by the car. I opened the door. Bauer would not see the movement from where he was and the salvage men had far too many trees to look through them.

'Get in on the floor,' I said.

She snaked in and curled on the floor at the far side of the front. I looked down the track the car headed into and saw that if I held the wheel dead where it was, I ought to get on down the road without running into a tree.

I got in, keeping right down and pulled the

door to. I reached up, got the bottom rim of the wheel, then started the motor and pushed the accelerator half down.

She didn't move, but when the brake was let off she did and in some fashion.

What the hell it looked like from outside, I don't know, but a driverless car making some speed is always a sure chiller to a passer by.

There was no firing but a lot of shouts.

I saw the tops of the trees flashing by overhead. They seemed to bow over us as we went on down the track.

Firing started. I did not know then if we got hit but what they were shooting for I don't know. The tyres are the only things you can be sure will upset things if one goes suddenly flat. They wouldn't have been able to hit one as the wheels bounced on that bumpy track.

I twisted and scrambled up into the seat. I had to let the accelerator go an instant as I took my hand off to get up and a good thing I did.

I came to the command of the ship just as we were going headlong for a tree on the right hand side of the road.

She came round when I wheeled hard over, but it was almost too sudden for the speed we had and we scrapped sideways on the dust and sideswiped the tree with a horrible crunch.

But we were away.

In the mirror I saw men in the road firing at us, but with pistols. The range was then too great for any hope of a hit, and the dust was kicking up behind us to make the aim more difficult.

'Don't ease up,' she said, scrambling up into the seat beside me. 'They won't give in, you know.'

So we kept going. Twice Kate turned me off the direct way back into other tracks, woodmen's tracks by the look of the pine chippings often piled by the side of the way.

'You didn't tell me the truth about coming to Karen, did you?' she said accusingly.

'Yes,' I said.

'Then you left something out. You came to Karen because you'd heard something was wrong.'

'Only that there was a funny sum of money which was quite unusual.'

'849,' she said.

I nearly went off the road then.

'How the devil do you know?'

'Because it isn't a sum of money at all. It's the number of a person. You knew that, didn't you?'

'It isn't a person's number – or it wasn't,' I said. 'I looked back through my grandfather's papers just to check if any unusual sums had appeared before.

'Twice before that number appeared. Now

the interesting part was that £849 now isn't much. But over thirty years ago it was a very large sum to spend redecorating a house. In fact, with a small house like this, almost impossible.

'And then I saw from his diaries that the number 849 was mentioned twice in them. After each entry he had come over for a visit. I didn't hitch on to this until I came and had a look myself just to make sure the £849 hadn't been spent. Pretty well nothing had been spent.'

'So you had an idea before you came that it was a signal?'

'No. I just noted my grandfather's visits and thought that he, like me, had merely come over to find what the hell it was all being spent on.'

'It was a signal meant to call you over.' She repeated her guess firmly.

'Well, it achieved it's purpose. I came, didn't I?'

'Tell me all about it.'

Throughout this short discussion we had been tearing along the forest tracks with never two seconds passing without a glance in the mirror to watch the dust cloud behind us.

I told her what had happened.

'Filthy business, that hand,' she said. 'Shuddery.'

Then she grabbed my arm and we almost

swerved into a pile of chippings.

'The hand, for heaven's sake! The hand!' she cried.

'What about it?'

'A man lost a hand by torture once, and it became the symbol of a group– Look out!'

I didn't need to be told to look out. A ten foot high tractor came swinging round the bend ahead of us dragging a long trailer of chained logs, each about thirty feet long.

The vast machine drew to a halt, its upright exhaust chuntering diesel fumes up into the summer air. A man peered down from the cab, and that was all he did.

I looked around me. There was no room to pass so it was a question of me getting out of the way. I backed, took a curve into the ground amongst the trees and cleared the way for him.

He gave no sign that he was grateful but just started his giant rolling forward. He got it so that the great train of logs was blocking our entire front and then he stopped.

'We've bitten it!' I said, opening the door.

I saw the vertical radio aerial on top of the tractor cab and had no doubt how he had been given instructions.

We got out. He did nothing, that driver, but sat up high above us, quietly smoking a black cigar. His window was shut. He made no attempt to open it and get down.

In fact, all he was going to do was sit there

until our pursuers came up to relieve him from further responsibility.

Kate got out and we started off into the forest at the back of the trailer. He might have seen us in his crab-eye mirrors but we dodged in and out of the trees pretty smartly until we reached a thicket on the slope of a hill.

There we stopped and looked back. The rumble of the idling diesel was soft on the air, but as we listened we heard the higher pitched sound of a car making some speed through the forest.

Peering through from our cover I saw the little VW come tearing up as if determined to destroy the giant in its path.

It stopped and the doors all fell open at once. Four men got out, but we were then too far away to see who they were.

They shouted up to the driver in his cab. He had opened the windscreen and yelled back down through the gap.

In jumping out of the car, I'd had the sense to grab the map and I had it now stuffed in my shirt.

From the time and the sun above the trees we could get a rough bearing and went on, following that heading for a mile or more.

Several times we heard faint shouts behind us, but they grew fainter, fewer and finally stopped. We were left with the birds and the rushing of a tumbling stream somewhere on the slope of the hill.

I found the stream on the map and got a fix from it when we saw it fifty yards to our left, tumbling over a rocky fall.

'It's going to be a good walk,' I said.

'I don't mind the walk,' she said. 'It's what goes in between round here that gives me goosepimples. They haven't given up, those hounds. We'll see them again, you bet me.'

'I won't,' I said.

And as we paused and listened to the birds and the stream I heard a gatheringly familiar sound, the sort of crickety haymaker sound of the VW exhaust.

And it didn't sound too far away.

2

There is something chilling about being followed by something you can hear but cannot see. Also, in that thick forest the sound kept echoing so that it seemed to come from one direction one moment, and from quite another the next.

'There's a track it might be going on,' I said, showing her the map.

The track went curling down the valley we were following, a valley of hills between mountains and then cut across ahead of us.

'If they're using that road,' I said, 'they know which way we're heading.'

'They know we must go back to Karen,' she said. 'Because what we want to know is there.'

'So all they have to do is wait on that road until we try and cross it, unless we do the Tarzan act swinging over the top in the trees.'

'I'm no female gorilla,' she said. 'I'll walk.'

We went on over a hill and down into a dip where the stream came winding along to our left and crossed our way further on. The cheerful hissing of the water killed the sound of the Beetle ahead of us.

We crossed it by jumping a large central stone and hopping the rest from there. She had no trouble. She could dance on a stone as ably as she could shie a block and hit Bauer in the ear.

On the other side we pushed on up the hill between trees until suddenly she stopped and pulled me in behind a big, dry looking bush.

'Up there!' she said, pointing.

For a moment 1 could see nothing but trees and bushes and mossy rocks climbing the slope of the hill. Then I saw a man move out – or rather a bundle of a man.

He stood, crouching like a hunchback, and raised an arm and beckoned. Startled I moved out of cover and raised a hand in query.

He raised his right arm and I saw steel

glint. My instinct was to duck from a shot, but the angle the steel took the light in was not like that reflecting on a gun barrel.

It was like light shining on a steel hand.

The spiderman stayed with it raised up for a few seconds, then beckoned again.

'It's our friend,' I said dryly. 'He means us to go up there. He saved me not long back. He might be a boy scout. We can't do worse.'

'Why not?'

I touched her shoulder and steered her to look round the bush and along the slope of the hill. As it ran down there was a break in the trees and we could see a piece of track.

Upon the track stood the Beetle, and four men around it, slowly scanning the hill.

'Okay,' she said. 'It's a choice of horrors.'

We started off up the higher part of the hill towards the spiderman. But as we did, he turned and scuttled off in amongst a dense mass of undergrowth.

'You said friendly,' she said, stopping.

'He beckoned,' I said. 'And he saved my skin. Come on.'

I needn't mention that we whispered for fear of our voices carrying in the echoing trees.

We clambered on up the slope and came to where I had seen him. It was different country. Not pinewood, but grass and more ordinary looking trees with plenty of leaves reaching down nearly to the ground.

We came into a small clearing amongst this vegetation and I stopped and looked round, expecting he would be there to welcome us.

Nothing moved but the leaves.

Kate pointed suddenly.

'Look! That piece of wood stuck in the ground.'

I looked to a piece of timber – it looked like a length of sawn off railway sleeper, stuck in the ground and green with moss and damp stain.

Letters, roughly cut in with a gouge, softened and shallowed by years, could still be read. It was a name.

'Heinz Drucke Immelmann, 1943.'

'We're not the first to have been hunted through this forest,' I said.

'Darling,' she whispered, pointing to the memorial. 'Heinz Drucke Immelmann. H.D.I. Do you see?'

'It means nil.'

'It was the name of an organisation which worked from Karen during the war.'

'Well, it looks as if it died then, too.'

'H is the eighth letter, D the fourth, I the ninth.'

'849,' I said. 'Well, well!'

'It operated from Karen,' she said. 'So somewhere here there is a way back to the cellar. You know about that, you said.'

I thought of the men down on the road

below and said, 'Let's get looking. It must have been this our friend wanted us to find.'

So we started looking. We didn't find anything until we had a second look at a big oak which had been split by some wandering storm of the past. The edges of the break were rounded off by years so that the edges were almost polished.

'Try that,' I said.

She slipped through the crack and into the tree.

'Anything?' I said, then wished I hadn't spoken.

For from down the hillside I could hear men's voices. It was quite sudden as if an order had been given and the answers returned, careless of who would hear.

'This is it,' Kate voice hissed back. 'Hollow right down. I'm just going to let go and fall. Bless me in case it's a pit of crocodiles down there.'

I heard a slithering and then a faint thud, then a gasp.

'Is it?' I whispered. 'Quick! They're coming up!'

'Come on anyway. The water's warm,' she hissed back.

I squeezed in through the crack and into the darkness. My feet had nothing underneath. My shoulders were wedged in the tree holding me up.

From outside the tree I heard a loud

151

shout. I wondered if they had found some track of us and if they had they would be peering in the tree very soon.

I could not see out and did not know how close one of them might be. For that reason I did not risk another thud and stuck where I was by bracing my muscles and feeling – very gingerly for a foothold at the sides of the hole below me.

Some quick talk happened without. I caught a word here and there and there was no doubt what it meant.

They had found prints on the grass somewhere near the timber memorial, and if not footprints, then marks of some kind we had left.

An order almost jubilant in tone, was barked out, following a snapped sentence which I understood.

'Now we have them!'

I just stuck where I was. There was nothing else to do. It was just possible that anyone sticking his head in this dark hollow in the tree wouldn't see me but it was quite the forlornest hope that ever came to my mind.

I heard them moving, no longer careful of being quiet. They moved away.

There was no doubt of this for the noises grew less instead of greater. In a minute I found myself still stuck in the tree with nothing more urgent than a cold sweat on my face, which threatened my sight.

I wriggled, contracted my shoulders and dropped. It seemed like falling ten thousand feet. My shoes dug in soft leaf mould and I tumbled forward on to all fours.

She whispered from out of the darkness.

'Are they there?'

'No. They went another way. I still can't believe it.'

'Perhaps it's your friend again. Perhaps he's a professional confuser.'

'And perhaps these chaps have no experience at tracking. Either way it's a welcome breather. Now what? Let's look around.'

My tiny torch for finding keyholes was in my key wallet on its usual hook. It was a pea in space. We had to hold it inches away from the earth walls, with their hairy fibres tangling out, to see anything at all.

The search seemed to go on for hours while constantly listening for any sound of the hunters returning above us. We didn't hear anything of them but in such a situation one should get no comfort from silence.

When we did find the exit it looked more suitable for a fox than a human. Low, just a ragged hole in the earth.

'Is that it?' she said incredulously.

'It wouldn't be obvious,' I said. 'From the very start its purpose was to mislead.'

'I hope it doesn't mislead us,' she said and

sat down on the earth floor. 'Goodbye, just in case.'

I got hold of her shoulders.

'Why are you so sure there's a way through to my cellar?' I said.

'I know there is, and I think this must be it.'

'Remember it's a tombstone that points the way.'

'Heigh-oh.'

She went. I followed. It was a rough ride, none of your stoutly built tunnels but a rabbit hole, sometimes three feet high, sometimes a foot, with trailing roots flicking our faces, dirt falling on to us in showers, sudden falls and just as sudden inclines. Sometimes we just slid down helpless, tangled up together, smothered in dirt. At others we clawed our way up what felt like soft earth cliffs, dragging the dirt down into our own faces.

I had the little torch fixed to my waistband, but it was useless most of the time. It helped once to dig her out with my hands when she got almost buried in a fall of dirt, but not much else.

'When does it end?' I said when we paused for a rest.

'At the end,' she said cheerfully and on we went.

Suddenly the floor rose up sheer and I felt her slipping down on top of me. I shoved her up again and we stood in a shower of dirt so thick I couldn't see anything.

'It's daylight up here,' she panted.

'Don't do anything rash,' I said. 'And keep dead quiet.'

The avalanche of dirt eased off and then I could see flickers of light as if leaves trembled and let it through. I pushed her up again.

'Okay,' she hissed.

'What can you see?' I whispered.

'Forest,' she said, in sharp disappointment. 'Perhaps it was a fox run after all!'

NINE

1

Kate crouched in what looked like a ring of bushes and peered around. I stuck my head up out of the hole and also took a look.

From the road we heard the Beetle start up again and chunter slowly along. The sound seemed to come from somewhere behind us.

There wasn't enough room in the bush ring for me to get up beside her without shoving her into a bush.

'See anything ahead?' I said.

'A cliff,' she said.

'That can't be right!' I said. 'There are cliffs to the west of the house, in which case we've headed the wrong way.'

She suddenly twisted and tumbled down head first on top of me. We went down together in the dirt below.

'Coming through the forest – two of them!' she hissed.

So we lay still a bit and heard heavy feet trampling somewhere just beyond the bushes.

When there was quiet again we disentangled and got up.

'This can't be right,' I said. 'It's a false trail. We must have missed the main line somewhere back.'

She agreed for once and we clambered back through the mould smelling darkness following the petrified pea of light almost with our noses on top of it.

We found another hole, quite a way back and crawled along it until I began to suspect it would never get anywhere.

The earth fell about us, some of the roots had grown so much since the original digging that we had to squeeze by their crooked fingers.

After what seemed an age she said, 'It doesn't look like a real tunnel. It's not a trap for nasty Nazis, is it?'

'We're too far now to turn back,' I said.

The tunnel got narrower, then smaller altogether. We began squirming along on our bellies, the luminous pea held ahead.

'It's coming to an end,' she panted, pulling my ankle.

'Don't let the dreaded claustrophobia grab you by the throat,' I remember saying. 'I can't breathe easily myself and panic is catching.'

'But it is, isn't it? Shrinking to a rat hole?'

'It's getting smaller,' I said. 'But is it because it goes nowhere, or that it was designed so that the unknowing would think it wasn't going anywhere?'

Soon after saying that I saw the small way ahead grilled by tree roots that seemed to bar any further progress.

'What's happened?' she said, as I stopped.

'There's a tree in the way.'

'I knew it,' she said. 'So what? Who stole the parachutes?'

I lay there prone or prostrate, whichever it is, and looked at the tangled screen of twisted roots. I hated those screwed up straggly bits. They made me mad.

When I get mad my impatient instinct is to shove through or try to. So I shoved hard to see if the roots were as strong as they looked.

And the whole damn lot – the whole twisted gnarled, knitted, sprawling network – pushed up to the roof.

'It opens!' I said and in my delight got a mouthful of crumbling dirt.

Spitting and tonguing out the dirt I wriggled on. The tunnel got even smaller, and but for the root barrier, I would have found my suspicions getting worse.

But the hole bent round and then opened out. I found I could get on all fours and crawl, then get up, bent double, and finally stand almost upright.

It was about then that the luminous pea came up against a much more solid barrier than the root screen. It was a stout wooden door, but it was nice to find this second proof of civilisation in the tunnel.

Moreover, the door wasn't locked. I pushed it in and some way off light shone, not daylight, but yellowish lights.

We closed the door. There were thick wooden bars inside and we shot these, too.

'It's your cellars,' she said.

'I hope,' I said.

We went on along a passage into the room where I had been with Munt and Lilli while the snowmen had prowled about the house above.

Remembering them made me remember the spy in the wall, and I crossed to it and pressed the button.

And it spoke.

'Who's that?' she whispered.

'It's somebody in the house right above us,' I said. 'Can you translate? I don't know much of it.'

She listened to a few sentences of conversation.

'It seems that they're dismantling a laboratory and taking it out to a truck,' she said. 'The fellow with the squeaky voice is directing the operations–'

I waited as she went silent and listened intently.

'When it's clear,' she said, 'they'll set fire to the place.'

'Indeed!' I said angrily.

She still listened.

'It's got to look like an electric fire.'

'There wasn't any juice when I left,' I said. 'I wonder if they know that?'

She went on listening and began to look puzzled. The talk became sporadic, but there were plenty of sounds of soft, shuffling feet going across the big room in the front of the house.

'What are they doing?'

'I don't know—' She grabbed my arm suddenly. From the speaker came some distant shouting, sounds of alarm and then a calling of orders from the big room.

'There's been an explosion. An oven or something,' she said. 'Somebody's been killed.'

Orders were barked.

'They're going to leave the body so it'll look as if somebody died in the fire,' she said.

'That's logical,' I said, 'but in my guess there's a body in that oven already. Keep me closely informed of what's going. I'm going to stop that fire but I don't want to run into a dozen geezers up there. I want the moment when most of them are out in the truck and only one or two are in the room up there.'

'I can't see through the floor,' she said.

'You'll have to take it by sound.'

I began to have a good look round then,

because it naturally occurred that if you have a hideaway from violence, you should somewhere have a small store of anti-violent material, such as a blunderbuss or similar deterrent.

I didn't expect very much, as I reckoned any such stuff would have been there many years.

There were cupboards and drawers in the furniture, but I found no iron comforts.

The other room was painfully bare except for the battery of batteries in the corner, though there were the cases of provisions standing about anyhow.

It was a possibility, so I began to look in the cases. Five of the ten wooden cases had loose tops and some of the tinned stuff was missing.

Then in an incomplete case of Heinz Tomato Soup I found two Lugers and a Mauser and a lot of loose ammunition just piled in between the cans.

I loaded up the Lugers after making sure the mechanisms worked. There is nothing more treacherous for the shooter than a rusty gun.

Back in the other room she was still at the listening post.

'They're having trouble,' she said.

'What sort?'

'I can't make out, but something's gone wrong upstairs.'

'Another explosion?'

I could hear the confused shouting in the speaker, but it meant only near panic to me.

'Perhaps the fire's started?' I said.

'If it has it isn't the one they meant.'

'While confusion reigns is the time to walk in,' I said, and gave her a Luger. 'Do you know how to operate it?'

She nodded.

'Okay,' I said. 'I'm going up. You cover the line from the opening as I go up through. Don't close it. Watch from there.'

Again she nodded and her eyes gleamed. She gorged on excitement.

We went through into the small room and up the steps under the table. It would be daylight up in the room so the tilting table must be moved very slowly so that men occupied with other things wouldn't notice it moving.

I raised it very slowly indeed until I could see out through the long slot into the room. I looked towards the door to the stairs and I saw a man in an asbestos suit on the flight, shouting something to a man standing quite near the table.

The man near me yelled back, and the man on the stair passed on the message upwards. There was a strong smell of some sort of chemical smoke which I couldn't identify.

I raised the table a little more. Nobody

seemed to notice.

From what I could see the whole of the operations were taking place upstairs. The man by the table moved forward to the door. There was a babel of shouting going on upstairs and a kind of tension I could feel in the air.

As if men above were fighting to stop the whole place blowing up.

'Can you tell what's going on?' I whispered.

'There's a panic on but they don't say what it is. Just shouting. Orders. Be careful. That sort of thing.'

The man at the stairs door turned round suddenly. He, like the others, was in his snow suit so that I could not see just where his eyes looked through the glass window in his helmet. I had the idea he was looking at the table which by then must have been noticeably tilting.

A wilder outbreak of shouting came from above just as the man started towards the table. He had a gun in his gauntleted hand.

I shot him through the shoulder so that he dropped his gun and half turned back towards the door under the impact.

While he did that I slipped out through the opening and got up as he went to start yelling through his microphone in the helmet.

I got him round the middle and threw him

to the ground and held him there so that the only sounds coming from his speech box was a lot of panting.

I gave him a thump in the wind and dragged him across the polished floor and outside. It was dusk, then.

Once out the job was easy. I got his suit off him, a big sloppy blanket suit that was put on like a tent.

I didn't know his face.

Just about then, when I was deciding to tie him up somehow, Kate came out behind me.

'All right. I'll keep him,' she said, looking up to the windows of the lab.

The uproar went on up there while I donned the space suit. I had dragged him half under a bush so he could not been seen from upstairs.

I turned and took a look at the waiting truck. The cab doors were open and nobody was inside. The tailboard was down and some crates and things had been pushed on board. There was no sign of anything else going on. The disaster, whatever it was up in the laboratory had taken everybody to it.

So I went as well.

2

As I walked into the house again I had a

fleeting wonder of what had happened to Bauer, Munt and Lilli. None of them seemed to have anything to do with the snowmen. Munt and Lilli were together and, I thought, honest. Bauer might be in with the phone tappers, but surely if he had been in with the snowmen, too, he would have been here now, directing the operations?

Nothing seemed to add up and I could not see then that it was all very simple. Things always are, afterwards.

It was stifling hot in that suit. When I got to the stairs door I heard the hubbub going on upstairs. Whatever the men were trying to do was working them into a state of near panic.

No one was on the stair now. The passer-on of messages had gone up to help the others.

I started up the flight and then saw someone in the open doorway of the kitchen. In the growing dusk I could not make out who it was. Also the angle of looking downward shortened the shadow.

What I could see was that the figure wore no asbestos suit.

At that moment the shouting above grew sharp and was followed by a brilliant flash that lit the whole staircase and the man standing down there in the doorway.

It was Munt and his attitude was very reminiscent of him when he had tossed the bomb into the tapping room.

For me, stopping him tossing any more was essential. In my uniform he didn't know me from the others.

I swung up and over the banisters and landed just ahead of him in the doorway. I stuck the Luger in his belly. He went stiff and obeyed my pushing by backing into the kitchen.

With my free hand I shoved the helmet off my head so that it hung at my back. He uttered a cry of astonishment.

'Don't blow me up,' I hissed at him. 'I might help!'

'You are one of them after all?' he said blankly.

'The hell no. I got this off one of them. I'm trying to find what they're up to.'

He caught my arm then.

'Don't go up there!' he hissed. 'It is death now!'

'From what?' I said.

'Extreme radiation. The fools have released it. It will disintegrate them!'

'Then what are they trying to do?' I said. 'Close the oven door?'

'You know, then? Yes that is what. But they will not get near. The fools! You cannot dismantle these things unless you know–'

I looked up. Through the top of the door-way on the landing there were blazing flashes of light, as if there should be bangs along with it, but none came. The sounds were of short orders, tense, and here and there a kind of sobbing curse.

'Could you close it?' I said.

'Not now,' he said. 'It should never be opened without it is run down for three days.'

'Why did you come back here?' I said.

'I had to see what they have done.'

In the flares of light from upstairs I could see his face running with sweat.

'How far will that radiation reach?' I said, seeing a man's helmeted head staggered back across the doorway up there.

'In a direct line from the oven. Practically no fan effect.'

I felt my own face cold with sweat and wiped it with my hand. Had he come back just to see, or did he intend to be sure the furnace burnt the whole house and the men in it?

It was difficult to grasp why they stayed up there fighting what they must have known by then was a hopeless battle. Why not run and let the house burn up?

I turned to simpler questions.

'Where's Lilli Braun?'

He hesitated and then showed his teeth.

'That is why I have come back. I do not know.'

'That's handy. But you must have an idea which gang has got her?'

'I think Bauer.'

'I've met Bauer. He is alone.'

The activity upstairs seemed to be getting less. I looked up again. The irregular flares of light had faded almost to a glow.

'They've got the door shut,' I said.

He shook his head.

'The glare is but temporary. The radiation gives little light.'

'I'm going to look,' I said.

And like a fool I started to go. Before I took the whole of one step something hard stuck me in the back.

'Do not go,' he said.

'I thought you were on my side,' I said.

'That is why I save you.'

'You just want to stay and let those men fry up there?'

'The world will be the better off without them. Do you know what they mean to do with my discovery? Make war with it. If they do that millions will die. So it is better that a few die now.'

Not much doubt about the moral side of that – providing Munt spoke the truth. In any case, with my back to him and a gun stuck in it seemed prudent to accept his view.

'Suppose the place burns down?' I said.

'It should not,' he said. 'It is not heat they have released.'

'Well, you know what it is. I don't. What

do you intend to do? Why were you waiting here?'

'To make sure that everyone went up there. You seemed to be the last of them. Then I would have gone.'

A thought struck me.

'Did you fix that oven for them?'

'I left it so that there would be no doubt that it would open when they began dismantling.'

It had got almost quiet upstairs. I began to feel rather odd and the more I tried to sort out in which order to think things out it just got all jumbled up.

'I'm going outside,' I said. 'It's too hot in here.'

'The back door please,' he said.

So we went out into the near darkness and the cool air made me feel better. It also made me feel I couldn't stand out there and let a half dozen men fry up in a laboratory.

But the gun still poked in my back, and having had a lot of experience, I knew there was no way to twist and turn the tables before the gun went off. When it is actually dug in the back the act of twisting or ducking could be enough to get the finger going from sheer shock.

'Look here, Munt,' I said. 'Leaving them is one thing. It may be justice. But the things they would tell the authorities might be more useful still. Have you thought of that?'

'I have thought of them dying,' he said, sharply, 'And I am still thinking only of that.'

'Cold blooded,' I said dryly.

'War is cold blooded,' he said angrily. 'Further there is the matter of Lilli, which you seem to forget.'

So it was Lilli. My earlier suspicions that they were lovers was confirmed. So long as she was in danger he was willing to let anybody roast. Not quite such a noble object as the preservation of peace, but more instantly understandable.

'If that's what you mean, then what are we doing standing out here?' I said. 'You can't find her if you don't look!'

'Where to look?'

And then a shocking idea occurred to me, and one for which I could not then find any reason. Perhaps it was an instinct set in motion by some small unnoticed detail that had been snatched by my subconscious only.

'My God!' I cried. 'In one of these suits! Quick! Get back in the house!'

I remember now with a weak feeling that I just started forward and forgot the gun in my back.

It didn't fire. His nerves must have been better than I had thought.

TEN

1

I heard Munt shout behind me.

'You are mad! Don't go! It cannot be–!'

I was in the back door by then and running fast despite the clumsy blanket suit. At the bottom of the stairs something made me halt. I stayed there a moment, listening.

There was no sound at all from upstairs. After the shouting and excitement that had been there before the silence was awful.

I went on up and to the door of the laboratory. The room and apparatus was partly dismantled, things overturned, everything apparently done hurriedly or without much scientific knowledge.

But now about the floor were five snowmen, all in odd attitudes. Some were sitting, backs against the walls or a bench, others just lay flat; one hung doubled over a trestle on his stomach.

There was no movement anywhere.

Instinctively, danger made me look to the great terracotta heater in the corner, expecting to see the red beam of Hell streaming from its belly.

There was nothing at all.

The furnace door was shut.

I heard Munt running below and went out to the landing.

'How many were here?' I said. 'Do you know?'

He stopped looking up.

'Five went up. One was on the stair, one out in the room.'

'Well, the one on the stair went up, so there should be six. But there are five.'

'Five?' he said and shook his head. 'No. It is six. Nobody came out by us at the back–' He stopped and looked into the living-room.

'What's missing?' I heard Kate's clear young voice say.

'A man ran out, perhaps?' Munt said.

'No man ran out,' said Kate. 'But there's a man who's passed out. I stanched his wound and he fainted out.'

She came to Munt at the bottom and looked up.

I went back to the door and surveyed the room again. Five men. The equipment had been sufficiently thinned out to let me see that no one was hidden.

With the Luger held at the ready I went into the bedrooms and looked round very carefully. No one was there.

There was of course the third way out known to very few. But it was known to Lilli. In the excitement of getting the captive who had now passed out, I hadn't forgotten to bump the tilted table so that it had shut.

The idea at the back of my mind had been so that we should still have a bolt hole the others wouldn't know about, and it would have been an open secret had we left the trap open.

Downstairs I went into the living-room and saw the table was properly shut down. Munt and Kate watched me.

'Are those men dead up there?' I said, turning on Munt. 'You'd better go and look.'

'But it is unsafe. I told you–'

'The furnace door is shut,' I said.

He stopped dead then.

'But that cannot be! No one could shut it! It was fixed–' Then he stopped as if he had given something away.

Or given somebody away.

Lilli would have seen him fix it, or known he had done it and probably how.

If this was correct, she had closed the door and gone. Which meant she wasn't on Munt's side and the theory of the lovers was hollow.

Munt turned and went away upstairs in one big hurry.

'What's the Master think?' said Kate.

'The Master's almost got past thinking,' I said. 'There was the choking sort of chemical stink when we first came in here and it fogged my head. Do you know anything that might help?'

'The snowmen and the exchange tapping is all one thing, spying,' she said. 'Most of the Eastern European main lines go through that jack box out in the forest.'

'It cost a lot of money, that tapper. Munt blew it up with a single pineapple. He must have known a lot about it to be wandering about there with such equipment. One doesn't normally carry the fruit for a walk in the forest.'

'You don't really know anything about anybody here, do you?' she said with a sweet smile. 'You turn up, find a woman who says she's your agent. She then says Munt is your ex-tenant. Who says so? She does. Nobody comes and sees them and says, "yes, that's them".'

'Very foolish of me,' I said. 'But I'm not a professional. Do you know more?'

'What brought you?'

'A queer sum and a wish for a holiday.'

'You checked and found that same sum had been written in twice before, though forty years divided the entries.'

'It was a funny coincidence, especially as Grandfather had come over each time the sum occurred.' I listened for a moment to Munt moving about upstairs in the room overhead. 'That must have been at the back of my mind, but really I like to try and think

I'm original.'

'And HDI is over forty years old,' she said, watching me.

'Do you mean they still work for the same interests? Through all that time?'

'What's changed in that time?'

We listened again. There was a lot of bumping up there. She went to the door and looked out.

'He's still out,' she said, puzzled. 'Can you faint that long?'

'I've never tried,' I said, and looked towards the stairs door as Munt appeared on the flight. I went towards him as he stopped half-way down. 'Well?'

'It is not radiation,' he said. 'They had suffocated.'

'Inside their suits?' I said.

Until then I had blamed the smell of smoky chemicals for my thickness in the head. But in fact, that thickness had come after the smell of chemicals. In fact it had come after I had worn the helmet a few minutes.

Kate came back across the floor. I struggled out of the floppy suit and took a look at the breathing apparatus hitched to the chest of the suit.

'I'm no chemist,' I said, 'but suppose I put a small tasteless smelling chemical in the filters in this thing, so that after a while you would start breathing CO_2. It would get worse the more excited you got.'

Kate smiled. Munt just stood there. His deadpan expression, which had always been noticeable, seemed to glaze right over then and harden up.

'Was Bauer amongst those five?' I said.

'No.'

'These suits were firesuits,' I said. 'But I believe they were adapted as anti-radiation suits. The white colour, the cotton content of the material, probably other things a scientist would know about and I don't.'

'It is all guesswork!' Munt shouted suddenly.

The outburst shocked, it was so very sudden. As if the veneer had cracked from inner heat and showed the madness or rage behind.

'When do you expect Bauer?' I said.

Kate's eyes sharpened as she watched Munt. The man himself froze over again.

'I do not know. He must come, but if I knew when I could beat him. He would not let me have that advantage.'

He sat down at the long table and put his gun on the polished wood in front of him.

'Where did the odd man go?' Kate said.

He shrugged.

'Perhaps I miscount when they go up.'

'But someone shut the furnace door,' I said.

'I do not know how it was done,' Munt said.

'Are you sure that they opened it?' I said.

He shrugged again but did not reply.

'Those flashes up there looked like the blasts of light I saw in the glass tubes during the storm,' I said.

'But there is no storm tonight!' he said.

'Surely there is a storage system?' I said. 'What would be the good of something that only worked when a storm was about?'

His face went blank again.

'Of course,' he said. 'There is a storage system. Yes.'

Kate looked round towards the stairs. So did I. Munt's hand darted to the gun.

Someone was walking on the landing.

Munt started to his feet.

'Stay there!' I hissed at him.

'Sit down again,' Kate said. She pointed her Luger at him.

He sat down slowly, his hand still on the gun. He withdrew it as she snatched and took the weapon out of his reach.

I went to the door and looked up the stairs. It was almost dark but at the top I saw the missing snowman, moving slowly, a ghostly robot in the gloom.

A ghost, in fact, with no head.

'I have a gun here,' I said. 'Come down.'

The ghost stopped at the head of the stairs.

'No Herr Blake. You come up. There is a lot to be seen.'

I recognised the voice but couldn't place it.

'I'm coming up.' I said. 'And the gun's on you all the way.'

'You could hardly miss my fat,' said the ghost and chuckled.

I was confident it was Bauer, but his voice was different from that I had heard in the open air. He stepped back a pace to let me on to the landing.

Then I saw his fat, rather dark-skinned grinning face which, by comparison with the stark white suit, hadn't shown up in the gloom until I had got close.

'The garagier,' I said.

'Please come with me, Herr Blake,' he said and walked to the door of the laboratory. 'These men are dead,' he went on, waving a hand towards them as if they didn't matter.

'I know,' I said.

'We are not allowed in this country to leave such remains lying in private houses,' he said. 'It would be correct to remove them in their own truck.'

'My God,' I said.

'I have Stein coming,' he went on, smiling. 'He usually cleans up here so he will find no difficulty.'

'How did you escape?' I said.

'I did not put a pellet in *my* air intake, Herr Blake. That would have been very short-sighted.'

'You take it so lightly. But this is wholesale murder of five men!'

'It was as kind as killing a sick dog,' he said.

2

'Where were you when I looked up here?' I said.

He pointed to the ceiling.

'In the roof. Did you never look there?' He cocked his fat head.

'I was going to, but something happened. Something's been happening ever since I've been here.'

'But that is why you came, ja? You did not expect nothing to happen?'

'I didn't think I was going to run into a collision of spy organisations,' I said.

'No collision,' he said. 'It was all organised, all planned.'

'They planned their own deaths?' I said.

'No, we did that. HDI. We fight for freedom always. For forty years and more, although things seem to change the continued threat to freedom never does. Nazis or Stalinists or bad government, they all come to choke the people some way or another. Divided, also, we have a case for relief of friends, even relatives. We are a very small party. Our fathers began it, grandfathers, even, and we carry on. It began as a great principle. It goes on – fighting.'

'Against what, this time?'

'A spy organization. They steal secrets and sell them. So we made a secret for them, and they came.' He chuckled softly. 'Dangle a prize in front of the greedy and they come from their holes in the earth. Then–' He snapped his fingers.

We heard the truck mumbling outside. The undertaker had arrived.

'What was the bait? The catching of static energy from storms?'

'Benjamin Franklin did that, I think. No, it was more than that. Frankenstein worked on it for many years – the real discovery, that is.'

'His name *is* Frankenstein?'

'Ja.'

'Then the man Munt?'

'A hack chemist who was put in Frankenstein's place,' the garagier said. 'We did not mind that. It showed they were in our trap even before the main body showed themselves.'

'And Lilli?'

'One of them, but I do not know exactly.'

'Where is the real Lilli Braun? She is my agent, you know.'

'When we know Munt is here, Lilli sends the bill to the lawyers in England, number, eight-four-nine pounds.'

'They didn't know what it meant.'

'It did not have to mean anything. It brought you.'

'Why was I wanted?'

'We need this house now more than ever,' he said. 'And we know from – enquiries that you are a good sport, as you say, and we think therefore that when you know of us you will sell.'

Stein started coming upstairs.

'Was I meant to be involved in this exercise?'

He shrugged.

'It was thought that men of your experience of involvement would then see what was going on and would have much sympathy.'

'Just tell me, how do you know this about me?'

'The girl downstairs. She said you were hell bent for trouble.'

'She is with you?'

'She helps between us and the English people with whom we sometimes have business.'

'There had to be somebody,' I said.

Stein came up.

'What do you propose to do with these men?' I said.

'They will have a decent burial,' the garagier said. 'Which is a good deal more than they've given to the hundreds they have murdered.'

'Where do they come from?' I asked suddenly.

'From the East,' he said.

'I see. It's underground war.'

'All the time,' Stein said.

And then I began to see something, but didn't mention it then.

'What was Frankenstein's discovery?' I said.

'He was experimenting on the cure of certain diseases by the use of astral radiation. No doubt in the future he will be successful, I am sure of that. But it was known he was at work secretly here, and we made it look more secret. Then we secretly spread the wind with the story that his war was not against disease, but against War. That he had devised a natural method of destroying weapons without himself using weapons. This was a very attractive proposition to the East, as you will see.'

He made a gesture towards the laboratory.

I stood aside then and went downstairs. Munt was still at the table, smoking a cigarette. Kate was there, too, stroking her chin thoughtfully with the muzzle of the Luger and watching Munt as if trying to believe something he had said.

'Beifeld 12,' I said.

He flicked his eyes towards me, but said nothing.

'That underground exchange belonged to

the men from the East,' I said.

He sat there quite still.

'You blew it up,' I said. 'You hid with me when they came here for the first time in their protective clothing. When they wanted to shake you very badly they sent a Yank and gave him your own number. Isn't that so?'

He kept still and silent.

'You're the man from the West,' I said. 'What our friends the HDI rather overlooked is that when you bait the East, it often catches the West as well. The Americans don't like to lose a trick.'

He eased a bit then.

'So where did you send Lilli?' I said. 'She is your – what do you call it?– accomplice?'

He nodded then.

'I don't know where she is,' he snapped out. 'That's the truth. They've got her somewhere. It's hell. I was very fond of her.'

'Was?' I said. 'Are you depressed? Why do you think she's dead?'

'You don't know these operators,' he said. 'The procedure is to capture the enemy, shuttle him across the frontier into the East and there dispose of the evidence. It goes on all the time. I thought you would know that.'

'I have heard,' I said, going to the front door. 'So let us get our chum out of his stupor and ask him for details.'

Munt laughed.

'You're crazy! He won't spill anything.'

I went out, picked up the last snowman and carried him in. When I staggered into the room with him Kate was ready with a wet towel and a basin of cold water.

The jerking of being carried in had half awakened him. Now we sat him in a chair and she sloshed his face with icy water. After a bit he groaned, and a little after that again he opened his eyes.

Kate held the towel in his direct line of vision and slowly wrung it out. The only sound was the falling of the drops on the floorboards.

She smiled and began to swing the wet, twisted towel like a club. He watched, and then swallowed. He had obviously seen the treatment before.

'Your men are all dead,' I said. 'Turn and look through that door.'

The mass corpse transport had started. Stein and the garagier came slowly down the stairs each carrying a dead snowman.

He did not seem surprised, but he swallowed a lot and then looked at the girl swinging the wet towel again. She lunged suddenly and flicked his cheek with the end of it. He jerked his head back, his eyes wide.

Munt stood up.

'Let me have the torture rag,' he said, coming round the table. 'I've had just lots of experience. Just lots.'

And he had, too. I turned away and tried not to listen to the stinging wet smacks and the grunts of pain.

And then it started to come out, breathless, panting, but even then an endless stream of terrified German. When he stopped for want of breath Munt stabbed a question in and then the interrogation really began, stabbing words drawing quick agonised answers.

I went to the door and lit a cigarette. It was dark. The juice had come back on and Kate had turned on some lights in the house, but not many. She had some respect for what was going on and obviously thought undertakers should have soft lights.

For this reason I couldn't see outside. I turned back for Munt had thrown the towel into the basin with a slap and slurp of water. He turned away and wiped sweat from his face.

'So we know what we need,' he said.

'Who killed Haynes?' I said.

'Surely you must know,' he said.

'We don't always know. You thought that man wouldn't talk.'

He lit a cigarette. Kate gave the prisoner a drink of water.

'How many Lilli Brauns are there?' I said.

'One,' Munt said. 'Your agent – and mine.'

'But the HDI say she was against them.'

'She was against what you call the Snowmen. She was not with HDI. You see, they don't know every damn thing.'

'If she kept her alliance with you secret, she must be good.'

'She is damn, damn good,' he said, suddenly grim.

'I've never met anyone like her. That is the thing which Bauer knows.'

'Bauer is with the East?'

Munt laughed then.

'With anyone who pays and is willing to have him. My side won't.'

'And he's got Lilli?'

'That's why I'm waiting, Blake. Just to see him and ask him.'

'What time like now?'

The voice, chuckling, came from the front door. We all turned at once. Bauer stood there with a pistol in one hand and a cigar in the other. He stood carefully to one side of the open door, so that anyone out in the garden would not get him from the back.

He cocked his head as the noise of the truck starting up came in the quiet night. Then he grinned and nodded.

'I have a bargain to make with you, Herr Munt,' he said affably. 'You give me Frankenstein and I'll give you Lilli Braun. Now, is that not a fair exchange for you?'

It was an unfortunate position. We were caught with our pants down and all three guns lying on the table, so that any attempt to get one would mean a bullet in the belly.

'It would seem good,' Munt said, 'but I have no Frankenstein.'

'You know where he hides, perhaps?'

'He hides behind you!'

The apparition of the spiderman in that dim lighting was frightening. He had hair all over his head and face and only the whites of his eyes and teeth showed.

And one other thing.

As he came in through the doorway from the darkness outside he slung his right hand at Bauer. Only it wasn't a right hand, it was some kind of mechanical steel claw which I had seen gleam in the sun out in the forest.

The steel fingers grabbed the gun in Bauer's hand. The gun fired into it and there was a small explosion as the bullet smashed up on to the steel.

Bauer started to yell and let the gun go. It fell. He backed against the wall and stood there, quite still.

'I change my bargain!' he cried. 'Lilli for me!'

The steel claw went for his throat but stopped as Munt roared.

'Leave him!'

The spiderman became still, then turned the big, hairy face to Munt. Munt went across to the captive.

'Where is she?' he snapped.

'Oh no!' Bauer said, and shook his head.

'Not here with all your friends and their guns! What kind of a bargain is that, Herr Munt? That is what you would call an American deal, perhaps. But, no. Call off the dogs and you have Lilli. Leave your gun, your friends and come with me. If you do not–' he shrugged and looked tearfully at the ceiling, '–poor Lilli. I would be so sorry–'

'Come on, blast you!' Munt said, furiously.

'Goodnight,' said Bauer and beamed on us. 'We shall meet again. I feel it in my heart.'

The two men went out. With his good left hand the spiderman pulled the plastic bag of hair off his face and head. Beneath there was the face of an ordinary, very tired man.

'You are the doctor?' Kate said.

He sat down and nodded.

'It shall not puzzle you longer. Munt pretended to join with the Snowmen, as you christened them, as a chemist, and they wished him to kill me, take my place and steal the results of my work to hand on to them. It was realised it might take him some days to be sure of what he was doing.

'Munt told me as little as he could, but he told me I must disappear or he would have to kill me to save himself. One cannot vanish, so I became something else. I had this old mask from an almost forgotten amateur ghost play, and with a natural deformity caused by having my leg broken as a form of torture, it is not difficult for me to move like some unfortunate animal. Having had my hand severed at the same time, the use of a steel claw makes it not so difficult to scale brick walls. Fingernails give way, you know.'

How he could be so calm at the recounting of such bloody suffering staggered me.

'But it couldn't have been your hand – that thing upstairs–' I said.

'But yes,' he said. 'It is mine, but not my own, you might say. I am proud of it. It is a new process in artificial limbs. I made it but had no time to start wearing it before my disappearance had to be accomplished. If I had taken it, you understand, they would have known I was not dead.'

It was a little while before Munt and Lilli came into the house.

'That bloody bastard!' Munt said. 'She was in the summerhouse. Your friend the garageman locked her in there to stop her getting in the way of the snowmen's activity!'

'Bauer didn't have her at all?' I said.

'He'd overheard her being locked in and cautioned. He didn't even know where this locking in was taking place. He told me the woodshed and went.'

'One must admire his nerve,' I said.

'And his skill at surgery,' Frankenstein said bitterly, and held up the steel claw.

189